YOU ARE SPIDER-MAN...

"Leave Hulk alone, stupid bug-man," growls the green brute. "Hulk doesn't like this place. Did bug-man bring Hulk here?"

"No, no," you say, trying to calm him. I want to get you out of here. How about being a nice Hulk and following the stupid bug-man?"

"Hulk go away with bug-man?" he asks. "Away from here?"

"That's right!" Just come along and—"

At that moment the door slams open and a platoon of Doctor Doom's guards run in.

The Hulk screams in anger. He turns to glare at you, his massive hands clenching into fists. "Bug-man lied! You try to trap Hulk!"

Now you're trapped between Doom's armed guards and a rampaging jade giant.

Do you try to convince the Hulk you're on his side? Or do you t̶a̶k̶e̶ ̶y̶o̶u̶r̶ ̶c̶h̶a̶n̶c̶e̶s̶ attacking Doom's m̶e̶n̶?

SPIDER-MAN

SUPER THRILLER

YOU ARE SPIDER-MAN
vs.
THE INCREDIBLE HULK

Richie Chevat

Illustrations by Ernie Colón

BYRON PREISS MULTIMEDIA COMPANY, INC.

NEW YORK

AN ARCHWAY PAPERBACK
Published by POCKET BOOKS
New York London Toronto Sydney Tokyo Singapore

This book is a work of fiction. Names, characters, places and incidents are products of the author's imagination or are used fictitiously. Any resemblance to actual events or locales or persons, living or dead, is entirely coincidental.

AN ARCHWAY PAPERBACK *Original*

An Archway Paperback published by
POCKET BOOKS, a division of Simon & Schuster Inc.
1230 Avenue of the Americas, New York, NY 10020

Byron Preiss Multimedia Company, Inc.
24 West 25th Street
New York, New York 10010

The Byron Preiss Multimedia Worldwide Web Site Address is:
http://www.byronpreiss.com

ISBN 0-671-00797-1

First Archway Paperback printing June 1997

10 9 8 7 6 5 4 3 2 1

Edited by Steve Roman
Cover art by Mike Zeck and Phil Zimelman
Cover design by Claude Goodwin
Interior design by MM Design 2000, Inc.

Printed in the U.S.A.

187189

CHAPTER 1

"**O**h, brother!"

You can't believe you did it! After all, you *are* Peter Parker, photographer for the *Daily Bugle*, aren't you? And you are on assignment covering an important press conference at the General Techtronics Corporation, aren't you? And what does a photographer need on assignment? How about *film*?

But of course, film is the one thing you don't have. You must have forgotten to pack the extra rolls when you left your apartment. You stand on the roof of the General Techtronics building, looking about helplessly. You're on the roof, of course, because in addition to being Peter Parker, you're also Spider-Man. You were a little late for the press conference, so naturally, you did a little webslinging to get here on time. And you made it with ten minutes to spare. But in the rush you forgot to pack your film. All you have is a few unexposed shots on the roll that's in your camera.

You look around, searching for a drug store, a candy store, a Film Is Us, anyplace

1

where you can buy film. But all you can see are the gleaming glass buildings and parking lots of the vast General Techtronics complex. And even though it's a warm spring day, the site of all that shiny glass and chrome makes you shiver as you remember an event that changed your life forever.

It was years ago, back when you were a nerdy high school student. You had been attending a scientific exhibition on the latest advances in the use of radioactive materials. The exhibition had been sponsored by GTC. What no one realized was that, during a demonstration, a spider had lowered itself into the equipment and become irradiated. As it was dying, it dropped from the equipment onto your hand and bit you. Soon after you discovered you had new, strange powers, powers that made you Spider-Man. In a sense, General Techtronics is responsible for turning you into a super hero.

And as usual when you think of that fateful day, you can't help wondering for a moment how your life would have been different if you'd never become Spider-Man. You wonder, what would I be doing now? Would I be a scientist? A photographer? Photographer!

You snap back to the present. The conference is starting in just a few minutes and you still don't have enough film. You could slip back into your Spidey costume and try to find a place to buy some film in the time you have

You stand on the roof of the General Techtronics building, looking about helplessly . . . you forgot to pack your film.

left. But you might not make it back in time. Or you could try to make do with the film you have.

If you don't get any good photos then your boss, J. Jonah Jameson, will take your head off. But he'll also kill you if you miss anything important. What do you do?

IF YOU GO BUY FILM,
GO TO CHAPTER 2, PAGE 17.

IF YOU GO STRAIGHT TO THE PRESS
CONFERENCE, GO TO CHAPTER 3.

CHAPTER 3

Quickly you run down the stairs from the roof, then grab an elevator to the main floor. The lobby is almost deserted, because everyone is already inside the conference hall. You can barely squeeze your way into the packed auditorium.

"This is more popular than a Pearl Jam concert," you think as you look for a good spot from which to take pictures. There's a large stage across the front of the hall and a deep blue curtain is drawn across it. Reporters, photographers and dozens of scientists fill every seat. You figure there are at least five hundred people there. No wonder Jameson wanted to get pictures. You push down the aisle and crouch on the side with a group of other photographers and cameramen.

On stage, someone has already started talking. You recognize Dr. Walter Langkowski, General Techtronics' new Director of Research. He also happens to be one of the world's top experts on radiation and its effects on humans. You've studied his papers, so you know that he has one of the sharpest minds around.

"Astronium!" Langkowski is saying. He's a tall, muscular man, with a creased and worried look on his face and closely-cropped blond hair. He's wearing a rumpled gray suit and his red tie is slightly off-center.

"If you've read the press kit," he says, "you know that astronium is a new element created here at General Techtronics. It's an element with a remarkable property unlike any other we've discovered. Astronium has the potential to revolutionize science. And that is because astronium *absorbs* radiation!"

Like the good science student you are, you *have* read the press materials, so you already know a lot of what Langkowski is talking about. And it's not all GTC public relations. Astronium *is* a pretty exciting discovery. It could make working with radioactive materials a lot safer.

But you also know there are some drawbacks to this new man-made element. First of all, there is very little of it. It's hard to produce because it is made from materials that are only found in certain asteroids. That's where the name Astronium comes from.

Second, and even more important, astronium is used in connection with radioactive materials. Handled incorrectly, it's possible for it to explode in a chain reaction.

You seriously doubt that Langkowski is going to mention any of those serious drawbacks; he doesn't. Instead, he presses a button on the lectern in front of him and the curtain across the stage begins to open. The other photographers around you edge forward, snapping their shutters. As the curtain opens, a spotlight is switched on somewhere in the back of the hall. Revealed in the light is a shiny machine, about the size of a van. It has banks of controls and two video screens built into it. You've spent a lot of time in laboratories, but you've never seen anything quite like this before.

Dr. Langkowski walks to the machine and places his hand on one of the keyboards. He turns to the crowd.

"This, ladies and gentlemen," he announces grandly, "is what we have brought you here to see today. This device, powered by astronium, was developed quite recently here at General Techtronics. It is the world's first Radiation Absorbing Deaccelerator. We call it R.A.D. for short."

The tall scientist punches some buttons on the keyboard and the R.A.D. springs to life. The control panels glow and pulse.

"We here at G.T.C. believe that the R.A.D. will once and for all neutralize the deadly danger of radiation exposure," he continues. "Of course, we are still a long way from testing it on humans. But we have successfully neutralized atomic radiation from spent nuclear fuel."

They really did it! If Langkowski is right, the R.A.D. will completely change the way the world thinks about radiation. Your mind races as you try to figure out its possible benefits to mankind. The only sound in the room is the whirring and clicking of cameras. The noise reminds you that you have a job to do and you elbow your way forward to take a few shots.

As you do, Langkowski continues talking.

"But before I go any further," he says, with a theatrical gesture. "Let me introduce the scientist who has done more than anyone else to make the R.A.D. a reality. In fact, it's safe to say that without this man there wouldn't *be* an R.A.D."

You're barely listening as you carefully count your shots, trying not to waste film.

But then Langkowski says something that stops your shutter finger cold.

"Ladies and gentlemen," he announces. "I'm proud to introduce my colleague and a scientist of world renown. The man who invented astronium—Dr. Bruce Banner!"

GO TO CHAPTER 4, PAGE 31.

CHAPTER 33

"Okay, let's give it a try," you say, trying to sound unconcerned. "After all, what do we have to lose? Just a few city blocks, more or less."

"There's nothing to worry about," Banner tells you as he leads you out of the laboratory and through a series of rooms.

"What, me worry?" you shoot back, trying to hide the fact that you're worried stiff.

But as Banner leads you into a large room and shows you his equipment, you begin to have some confidence. He is, after all, a brilliant scientist. And as he explains the process to you, it all makes sense. It really *ought* to work, right?

"The process involves a strong magnetic field," he says, showing you the robotic arms that will handle the used astronium. "Once the material is inserted into that chamber, I will begin." He points to a small compartment in the machine.

"I've built in a safety mechanism," he continues. "If for some reason a chain reaction does start, *this*," he pats a small computer that is wired into the main console, "will shut the whole thing down in time."

"Yeah, right," you think. "When do we put on our seatbelts?" you quip.

"No time like the present," he replies with a grim smile.

He presses some buttons and you feel the hum as the machinery springs to life. The robot arms begin to move. The small particle of astronium is placed inside the chamber.

"This is it," Banner says excitedly. "This is where we see if it works."

Naturally, it's exactly at this point that you hear the sound of gunfire and explosions nearby.

"What is it?" Banner shouts, not daring to look up from his computer screen.

"One guess!" you reply, bracing yourself.

The door to the laboratory blows inward at that very moment. You try to shield Banner, who stays glued to the controls.

"Shut it down!" you yell as a cloud of black smoke billows in through the wrecked door.

"I can't!" Banner yells back. Sweat is streaming down his face. "Not now!"

You don't have time to argue with him, because just then six Doctor Dooms appear through the dust and smoke.

"Doom sent them!" you think. The robots spot you at that instant. They turn in your direction. You know they're about to fire at you. You know you should dodge or leap away. You also know that Banner won't or can't leave the experiment.

You have just enough time to grab a heavy table and flip it over. You can only pray it will shield the two of you from the blast that is about to come.

Baroom!

The twin blasts of sonic cannons splinters the table like a matchbox. But it must have taken the brunt of the blast, because somehow you're still standing. You're feeling pretty lucky. You're also trying to figure out what to do next. Then you hear a terrible cry of pain from behind you.

"Arrgh!"

It's Banner. He's been hit by a flying splinter of wood that's wedged in his upper arm. Blood is spurting out and running down his lab coat. But that's not what frightens you. The wound isn't that bad. It's the look of wild anger you see in Banner's eyes. You know that look. His blood pressure is going up. His adrenaline is pumping. Another sec-

"This is it," Banner says excitedly. "This is where we see if it works."

ond or two and the process will start that will turn him into the incredible Hulk.

If you get him away now, there's a chance you can calm him down before he transforms. But that would mean leaving the experiment running untended. What if it goes wrong? On the other hand, if Banner turns into the Hulk, he's not going to be too good at physics anyway. Then it would be up to you to stop the experiment. And just to add to the fun, you've still got Doom's robots coming at you. What do you do?

IF YOU GET BANNER AWAY FROM HERE GO TO CHAPTER 34, PAGE 136.

IF YOU STAY AND TRY TO STOP THE EXPERIMENT, CHAPTER 35, PAGE 73.

CHAPTER 9

"I'd better not go near Banner," you tell yourself. "He's already upset. I don't want him to snap and become the Hulk."

You turn your back on the frantic scientist and face the two chrome-plated machines.

12

They're like something out of a bad Japanese monster movie, you think, and it'll probably take Godzilla to defeat them.

"Hey, bucket o' bolts," you quip to the nearest one. "How about taking this outside?"

But you've already sprung into motion. Your right hand shoots out, sending a spray of webbing from under your wrist to what you think are one of the robot's electronic "eyes." A split-second later you've dived forward into a roll. You bounce up with both feet aimed at the second robot's "stomach." But instead of a resounding thud which you hoped would send the metal warrior sprawling backwards, all you hear is a tiny:

Ping!

"Ow! That smarts!" you mumble as you bounce harmlessly off the steel-reinforced side of the robot.

Things move even faster. You dodge another energy burst while trying again to "blind" the robots with webbing. But they must have infra-red scanners or radar or some other way of getting around because it doesn't stop them. You hit them full force and they don't budge. And all the while, you hear Banner yelling something at you.

"Get out!" he's shouting. But is he talking to you, to the robots, or to the whole world? You don't have time to ask.

Quickly you scan the room for some kind

of an alarm. That's your first and only mistake. Too bad one is all you get. You took your eyes off the robot in front of you for one second too long. Now it has you pinned to the floor with a long steel arm.

"Get off me, you recycled washing machine!" you grunt. But your sparkling conversation doesn't have any effect.

"Get back! Get back!" you hear Banner shouting. You twist your head around in time to see the second robot grab the scientist in a metal claw.

"Uh-oh!" you whisper. "Big mistake."

You've seen it before, but it's still a fearful sight. In a matter of a few seconds, the average-sized Bruce Banner swells and morphs. He twists and grows in what must be very painful rapid changes. His skin turns a sickly green, his eye swell and bulge, his clothing splits at the seams. In another moment, you know there will be nothing left of Bruce Banner. You brace yourself for the appearance of the massive form of the incredible Hulk. Nothing you know of can stop his brute strength and almost unlimited power.

But just as you think, "Bye-bye robots," and add to yourself "Bye-bye General Techtronics and one little ol' Spider-Man," the transformation stops! You catch a faint whiff of something. Gas! It's coming from the robot holding the Hulk. And it's putting Banner to sleep—before he can complete his transformation.

As quickly as the change began, it reverses itself. In a moment the being in the robot's grasp has resumed the form of a sleeping, almost peaceful, Bruce Banner.

"Whoever sent these tin cans was prepared," you think. "They were after Banner."

Then you smell the gas again. Only this time it's coming from the robot holding *you*. You know you only have a few moments of consciousness left. Already the room is beginning to spin. Your arms and legs feel numb and disconnected. As the strength flows out of you, you manage to reach into your belt and pull out a tiny spider-tracer. The last thing you remember is attaching it to the back of the robot's leg.

You wake to the concerned and puzzled face of a GTC security guard.

"Hey, he's coming around!" he calls out. "Stay there, Spider-Man," he urges you. "I'll go get the medics." He runs out of your field of view.

"Medics? Gee, that's nice," you think groggily. Then it all comes back to you in a flash. You bolt upright and a searing pain shoots across your temples—a side-effect of the gas. But you shake it off and stumble to your feet. Tripping over the shambles that's left of the office, you drag yourself to the hole where

15

the wall once stood. Somewhere out there, someone has kidnapped Bruce Banner. And you're going to find him.

GO TO CHAPTER 15, PAGE 121.

CHAPTER 42

"Bug-man hurt Betty? Hulk hate bug-man! Hulk will smash bug-man!"

"Now, Hulkie," you stutter, trying to think of what to say.

How can you convince the Hulk that it's not Betty Ross? You can't even convince him that you're not a real bug!

The green monster lowers his head and charges you, his giant fists held out like twin battering rams. You leap easily out of the way and he flattens part of the wall behind you. In fact, he keeps going through three more walls before he slows down. At this rate, there won't be any of General Techtronics left standing by lunch time.

"Don't you like my new friend?" Doom taunts you. He's obviously enjoying himself.

Friend! If you could only show the Hulk

that his "friend" Betty was really a robot. You hear him charging back toward you, tearing apart the building as he comes. Suddenly, you have an idea. You can easily show Hulk that "Betty Ross" is just a robot. All you have to do is knock it open and show him the electronic parts inside. Even a dim bulb like the Hulk should catch on then. Wouldn't he? It just might work.

Do you try it?

IF YOU DO, GO TO CHAPTER 43, PAGE 102.

IF TRY TO THINK OF SOMETHING ELSE, GO TO CHAPTER 44, PAGE 58.

CHAPTER 2

"These things never start on time," you think. "If I'm really fast, I'll just miss the boring introduction speeches."

Quickly, you change back into your Spider-Man costume and run to the edge of the roof, ready to leap into the air. Then you stop. Which way should you go? There must be someone who knows how to get to the nearest convenience store. Then you spot a man and a woman walking in from the parking lot. They're almost directly below you and by the looks of it, they're engaged in a heated argument.

"I'll just drop in on them and ask directions," you think. Drop is the right word for it. You just step off the edge of the ten-story building and drop like a stone, straight down. To someone watching it would look like you're going to splatter yourself across the pavement. But at the last minute you shoot out a web-line that catches on the building. You bounce to a halt a few feet above the ground.

The couple are so involved in their discussion that they don't even notice you hanging upside-down above them. You think you recognize them from the GTC promotional brochures. They're two of General Techtronics' top researchers. They stop on the steps to the building and continue their argument in hushed tones.

You're about to interrupt them with a witty remark (or maybe a *Hey!*) but then you hear something that makes you hold your tongue.

"The used astronium is so dangerous," the woman is saying, "It's unstable! How can they produce more of it?"

Astronium! That's the new man-made element that GTC has developed. The press conference is supposed to announce a major breakthrough in astronium research. But you hadn't heard that it was really dangerous. Now your attention is riveted on the two scientists.

"They say they're building safety controls into the system," the man replies.

"Yes," the woman shoots back, angrily. "If they don't cut corners to save money. The only thing that seems able to control astronium is a *very strong magnetic field*. Besides, we all know that even the best safeguards sometimes fail."

"Well, let's hope they do it right," the man says as the two of them turn toward the front door. "Because if there was ever an astronium chain reaction, this whole part of the city would be burnt toast."

The two scientists disappear through the front doors. You hang there for a moment, digesting what you've heard. *Astronium. Chain reaction. Strong magnetic field.* The words echo through your mind.

"I wonder if they're going to discuss this at the press conference," you think, still hanging there.

Press conference!

Suddenly you remember why you're there. There's no time to go for more film now. You'll just have to make do with what you have. Quickly you swing your way back up to the roof and change back into your Peter Parker duds. Then you rush into the building to find the press conference.

GO TO CHAPTER 3, PAGE 4.

CHAPTER 19

You can't take the chance. Although Banner has never attacked you before, there's something really strange about the way he's been acting. Maybe Doom has hypnotized him.

All these thoughts flash through your mind in the time it takes you to drop Doctor Doom, leap across the room to Banner and grab the scientist's arm.

"Gotcha!" you cry, holding his hand up and snatching the—*medicine bottle?*

"What is this?" you ask, totally confused.

Banner looks at you with a mixture of fear and anger. "My tranquilizers!" he says. "To keep me from turning into the Hulk."

"Tranquilizers? What a relief!" you say. "I thought you were . . ."

As your spider-sense goes off, you realize it's too late to move. Banner was never a threat. The real threat was always the maniac who is now standing right behind you, the one who is about to—

You get clobbered pretty good. And when you wake up some time later with a headache the size of California, you have to admit you deserved it. You should have known Banner would never attack you or help Doom hurt other people. Now you're paying the price. You're strapped to a table deep inside one of Doom's dungeons. The fearsome-looking steel mask is right above you, only inches away.

"Spider-Man," he growls. "I'm so glad you have decided to stay. What made you change your mind?"

"Uh, the continental breakfast?" you wisecrack. But it comes out a little weakly. You know the only thing that's going to get cooked around here is you.

THE END

CHAPTER 29

Time is up.

"Bug-man tries to trick Hulk!" the Hulk screams. "Hulk smash!"

The Hulk storms toward you, waving his fists. You know that each one of those mitts can hit harder than a hundred tons of TNT.

"There's no way to explain this to him," you realize as you swing out of his way. "I don't even think he knows what a robot is. I'd better get out of here—only how?"

You're in a stone dungeon, under Doom's mansion, surrounded by Latverian guards and being chased by the incredible Hulk. Escape doesn't seem very likely. Well, you've gotten out of tougher jams before—even if you can't remember when.

"Stupid bug-man!" the Hulk scowls, as he clumsily tries to catch you. You leap out of his way again and again. "Hold still! How can Hulk smash if you move around so much?"

He comes toward you, and throws a punch in your general direction. Of course you dodge it in time, but the Hulk's fist keeps going.

Bam!

With a sound like a freight train hitting a mountain, the Hulk's fist tears through the stone wall of the dungeon. A shower of brick and steel falls to the floor and suddenly you see the night sky through the hole.

"Hulkie!" you shout. "You sure know how to make an exit!"

You swing over the mighty green monster and leap through the hole.

"Bug-man!" the Hulk shouts up at you. "Come back so Hulk can smash you!"

"Uh, no thanks," you say. A few running steps and you're at the embassy wall. One leap takes you over it. Now you're back in the sky, web-slinging into the safety of the darkness over the city. You've escaped, but you know that you're not done dealing with the Hulk—or Doc Doom.

GO TO CHAPTER 41, PAGE 77.

CHAPTER 20

Banner may be acting weird, but he'd never attack you. He's *never* done anything to hurt anyone, at least not as Bruce Banner. You finish up with Doctor Doom, using a good amount of webbing to securely tie him up.

"There you go!" you say, stepping back. "One tin-plated dictator, gift-wrapped and ready for delivery. You must be getting old, Doomsy, because that was easier than even I expected."

"Was it really?"

You have trouble not leaping out of your skin. The raspy voice coming from the doorway belongs to none other than Doctor Doom. The *real* Doctor Doom. You suddenly get the picture. The figure bound helplessly on the floor isn't the real Doom but another Doombot. No wonder he was so easy to defeat.

You try to maintain your composure as you turn to face the real Doom. At least, you *think* it's the real one. Things are starting to get a little confusing.

"Hey, a Doombot!" you say, trying to sound sure of yourself. "I knew it all along. Sure I did. You didn't have me fooled one bit."

"You lie!" Doom snaps. He's never cared for any of your jokes. "Your pitiful intellect is no match for my genius!"

"Some genius," you say. "Even a foreign dictator—uh, sorry, I mean diplomat—can go to jail for kidnapping."

"Kidnapping?" Doom laughs. "Who has been kidnapped?"

You jerk a thumb in Banner's direction. "Did you forget your robot attack on General Techtronics, Doom? The way you carried off Dr. Banner? There are hundreds of witnesses."

Doom waves his steel-gloved hand, dismissing your argument.

"You have no proof that those were my robots," he says. "And as for Dr. Banner, he's here as my guest."

You turn to Banner. To your amazement, he nods his head in agreement.

"It's true," he says, after a moment's pause. "I'm here of my own free will."

You try to think of something sharp to say, but all that comes out is, "What?!"

You turn back to Doom. "What did you

do to him, Doom?" you demand. "Hypnotize him?"

"Don't be so dramatic," Doom replies. "He merely sees the logic of working with me. Not everyone is as small-minded as you."

"It's true, Spider-Man," Banner interrupts, sounding weary. "He didn't do anything to me. Now please leave."

"You heard him, cretin," Doom gloats. "And do you also hear that?" In the distance is the unmistakable sound of police sirens, getting closer every second.

"They're coming to arrest you," Doom laughs. "For trespass! And destroying Latverian property!"

You glance around the wreckage of the room and your heart sinks. Somehow Doom has out-maneuvered you. He can make it look like you're the crook here. You have no choice but to get out of there fast.

"Okay, Doom," you say as you step to the edge of the ruined balcony. "You win this round. But this isn't over. I'm going to find out whatever you have on Banner. And when I do, I'll be back!"

You launch yourself into the night determined to carry out your threat. But all you hear is the sound of Doom's laughter echoing in the darkness.

GO TO CHAPTER 41, PAGE 77.

CHAPTER 47

You try to think fast. Where would the real Doom be headed? The astronium is right here. But there isn't very much of it. To make more, Doom will need the rare meteorites. And *those* are stored in the next building—the one the third Doom is headed for.

"That one!" you shout to the Hulk, pointing to the third Doom.

You shoot a web-line to the roof of the next building. As you jump into space, you feel a rush of air beside you. The Hulk has launched himself into the air, using only the force of his mighty leg muscles. You both land at the same time. Doom has disappeared inside. You head for the door. The Hulk grabs the corner of the glass and chrome building and is about to pry it open like a packing crate.

"Hulk, wait!" you shout. He looks at you innocently.

"Hulk will catch Tin Man!" he says.

"Yes," you nod. "But use the door, okay? And make sure you get the *real* Tin Man, right?"

The Hulk looks puzzled but shrugs and follows you through the door. You rush up the stairs, with the Hulk thundering behind you. The meteorite pieces are kept in a vault on the second floor. The two of you race down a hallway and into a large open space. The vault is on the far side. And in front of it is Doctor Doom. The huge door to the vault is already open.

Doom darts inside. For a moment you think you have him trapped. All you have to do is slam the door to the vault shut. But before you can cross the room the masked madman leaps out of the vault again. This time he's carrying a large vacuum chamber. He's got the meteorites!

You realize that he's off-balance, carrying the large chamber. Now is your moment. You launch yourself toward him before he can drop what he's carrying and fire at you. But just as you spring into your leap, the Hulk rushes past you. He just brushes you, but the force is enough to knock you sideways. Instead of clobbering Doom, you fall in a tangle at his feet. Doom jets upward and the Hulk crashes into the solid steel vault.

Bam!

The Hulk hits the foot-thick steel wall and makes a dent the size of a New York City pothole. Then the green goliath bounces off and falls—on you! The air is forced out of you and you can barely breathe. Plus, you think something may be broken. But there's no time to worry about that now. Doom is getting away with the meteorites! He's hurrying toward the door.

"Good-bye, fools!" he calls over his shoulder.

"Stop him!" you croak, your voice barely a whisper.

"Bug-man talk funny," the Hulk complains. He slowly picks himself up off of you. Now you can breathe.

"Get him!" you gasp. "Stop Tin Man!"

The Hulk doesn't need to be told twice. Like a mammoth green sprinter coming out of the starting blocks, he races after the cloaked figure. But he hasn't taken two steps when a *second* Doom steps out of the vault. This one is empty-handed.

"Hulk, you dim-witted monstrosity!" the second Doom cries. "Here I am! You're chasing a robot!"

The Hulk skids to a halt. He whips around and looks back and forth, completely confused. You're still recovering from being crushed by the Hulk and can barely pull yourself to your feet. Meanwhile, the second Doom runs to a nearby wall and, raising his steel gauntlets, blasts a hole in it.

The Hulk stands frozen.

"Bug-man say get real Tin Man!" he bellows "But which is real Tin Man?"

You don't know which one is the real Doom. But the important thing is to get the

In the rubble you find what's left of the Doombot.

meteorites. You try to raise your voice to tell the Hulk, but you can't catch your wind. Now the second Doom is standing in the jagged hole, ready to flee. The Hulk has to act now, and he has to make the choice on his own. He turns around and with a fantastic leap, grabs the first Doom as it disappears through the doorway. There's a blast and a bright orange flame and then you black out.

The next thing you know, someone is shaking you violently. You come to and find you're still lying by the vault. The Hulk is standing over you, poking you with one huge green finger as gently as he can manage.

"Bug-man!" he asks. "Are you dead?"

"No, Hulk," you gasp. "I don't think so."

In the rubble you find what's left of the Doombot. It exploded when the Hulk grabbed it. But the container with the meteorites is safe.

"Where's Doom?" you stammer.

"Tin Man flew away," the Hulk says. "Hulk is sorry."

"No, Hulk," you say, hauling yourself upright. "You did the right thing."

"Hulk did good?" the green giant says, with a goofy grin on his face.

"Yes, Hulk," you answer. "Hulk did good."

"Hulk feels good!" he shouts. "Hulk feels so good, Hulk not smash stupid bug-man!'

"Thanks, Hulk," you say. "That really means a lot to me."

GO TO CHAPTER 48, PAGE 85.

CHAPTER 4

Bruce Banner! You almost drop your camera in surprise. There's an audible gasp from the crowd that tells you a lot of other people are surprised, too.

You watch in shock as an ordinary-looking medium-sized man strides across the stage and takes his place next to Langkowski. He's wearing a white lab coat over a neat blue blazer. His brown hair is cut close and his angular face is fixed in a forced smile.

If you'd never seen him before, if you didn't know who he was, you'd think he was just another mild-mannered scientist. But you *do* know who he is. In fact, you know him only too well. And he's not at all what he appears to be. For you and everyone else in the hall knows that Bruce Banner is a man who can change—change into a destructive, uncontrollable beast, one with the power of a force of nature and just as unpredictable. You know that Bruce Banner is not just a man, he's also the Hulk!

What is Bruce Banner—the incredible Hulk—doing working with radioactive materials? After all, it was an overdose of gamma radiation that changed Banner into the Hulk in the first place. Now he's like two beings trapped in one body. Usually, he's Bruce Banner. But if Banner gets agitated, angry, or worked up for any reason, he transforms into the Hulk in a matter of seconds.

As if he can read your thoughts, Banner stands with his feet apart and almost glares out at the crowd. The talking and whispering starts to drown out what Langkowski is saying.

"People! Please!" The scientist pleads with the people in the hall. "Dr. Banner has been a valuable and, uh, stable member of our research team for some months now. Much of the work on R.A.D. is based on his research. Now, if we may, we'd like to proceed with the demonstration."

"Dr. Banner!" Jenny Chun, a reporter from one of the local television stations, has jumped to her feet and is addressing Banner. "Has working closely with astronium had any effect on your . . . monstrous alter-ego?"

"The Hulk is not a monster," Banner replies. He seems calm enough, but there's an edge in his voice.

"But have you felt *any* side effects?" the reporter presses on. "What if you were to become the Hulk while working on the project?"

Langkowski grabs the microphone.

"Please!" he insists. "Let me assure you. At no time during his work here has Dr. Banner's . . . unique condition been a problem. Now the R.A.D. is a remarkable device, which—"

"Dr. Banner!" This time it's a reporter from an out-of-town newspaper. "How can you be sure that the Hulk is under your control this time? How do we know he won't go berserk and destroy the project?"

Luckily, Banner seems to have his famous temper under control. At least for the moment. His face is red, but he just grits his teeth.

"You vultures!" he spits out. "This is what I thought would happen. You're not interested in science or progress. All you want is a juicy story. Well, I'm not giving it to you!"

With that, he turns on his heel and stalks off the stage. From your spot on the side of the room, you can see him slam open a door backstage and kick over a chair that's in his way. Then he disappears through the doorway.

That's not good, you realize. Just a little more of that and Banner would definitely "Hulk out." He probably left because he felt himself getting angry. Maybe you should go after him and make sure he calms down.

But if he was in control enough to leave,

he should be able to calm down on his own. After all, Langkowski said that Banner has been working on the project for months without turning into the Hulk. And you still have a job to do. Every other paper in town has a photographer there and Langkowski is about to go on with the demonstration. Jameson will kill you if you don't get a photo for him. You can't afford to mess up this assignment.

Still, Banner looked pretty bad. You don't know what to do. Should you follow him? Or stay for the R.A.D. demonstration?

IF YOU FOLLOW BANNER GO TO CHAPTER 5, PAGE 53.

IF YOU STAY, GO TO CHAPTER 10, PAGE 69.

CHAPTER 7

There's definitely something wrong with Banner, you realize. No reporters should be able to get him this worked up. You'll just have to chance it that you'll get back to the press conference in time to grab a couple of photos.

"I'd better follow him," you think as Banner disappears behind the security door. "As Spider-Man."

Luckily, there's a bathroom just down the hall. You slip into it unnoticed. A few moments later you're in your Spider-Man costume, and your camera bag is hidden inside a ceiling panel, secured with some webbing.

You come out of the bathroom and head for your favorite Spidey-path—the ceiling. Crawling along upside-down, you make your way back to the security barrier. Luckily, the guard's eyes are glued to a security monitor in front of him.

"I wonder if he gets *Oprah* on that thing?" you think as you pass noiselessly over his head.

Soon you've slipped though the door Banner went through and you're running silently down a long, deserted corridor. Everyone must be at the press conference, you realize. You figure Banner has headed back toward his lab or his office. But where is it?

"There must be a nameplate or a sign somewhere," you think, as you search for the scientist. Just then you hear his voice. It's coming from an open doorway just ahead. And he sounds every bit as angry as when he left the auditorium.

You slide up the wall until you are perched just beside the open door to Banner's office. Even if he wasn't shouting, you could hear him quite clearly. He must be talking to someone on the phone, because you can only hear his side of the conversation. And from the sound of it, the person he's talking to isn't one of Banner's favorite people.

"No!" he yells. "I told you before! How many times do I have to tell you? Why don't you leave me alone?"

This must be what is really bothering Banner, you realize. Someone is putting pressure on him. But who? And what kind of pressure? You wish you could hear what the person on the phone is saying, but all you can do is hang there and try to pick up whatever you can.

You lean down, your head almost in the doorway, and as you do, your spider-sense—which gives you split-second warnings of danger—starts buzzing like crazy. You don't have more than a nano-second to react. But you don't see or hear anything. Without thinking, you leap off the wall, and land standing up—right in Banner's doorway.

"Spider-Man!" he shouts. And he doesn't seem happy to see you.

You'd like to come back with a snappy reply, something like "Hey, Doc! I heard about the new job, and I thought I'd drop by and find out if you'd give me a tour of the place." But you don't really have time because at that same instant the outer wall and window to his office suddenly explode inward!

Sunlight comes in through the gap—and so do two very large, gleaming chrome robots.

Sunlight comes in through the gap—and so do two very large, gleaming chrome robots.

They're human in form, except that each is about eight feet tall. They seem to be outfitted with jet thrusters where their feet would be and some sort of energy field projector glows on each one's chest.

"Uh-oh!" you murmur. "Something tells me they're not delivering pizza."

They couldn't be here for you—they must be after Banner. You turn toward him, to warn him to run, but in the same instant, he turns to you.

"What is this, Spider-Man?" he shouts. "Can't you people leave me alone?"

"But—but—" you stammer. Banner thinks the robots are working with you!

"Why can't you just leave me in peace?" he shouts, jumping to a computer work station a few feet from his desk. "The minute you heard I was here, you had to start hounding me! You want to see if I'll become the Hulk. GTC will have you in jail for this!"

"But I didn't—" you start to say. You're cut off because the two robots are moving in the scientist's direction.

"Bruce Banner," a recorded voice says, quite pleasantly. "Please come with us. Do not attempt to resist."

"Go away!" Banner shouts. "All of you!" His hands are furiously punching keys on the computer terminal. Maybe he's sending a message for help.

You somersault over the nearest robot, and land standing up directly in its path.

"Banner!" you cry. "Get out of here! Move it!"

"Go away!" he shouts again. "I'm warning you!"

The scientist seems confused. His face is red and the veins on his neck are bulging. He could start transforming into the Hulk at any moment. What's worse, he seems to think you have something to do with the robot attack.

The robots have stopped for the moment. But aside from that they don't seem to notice you at all.

"They must be waiting for instructions," you think. "I wonder who's controlling them?"

It doesn't really matter. They're not going to stand there like that forever.

You have to move fast. Only what should you do? You could try to grab Banner and get him out of there. Only that might push him over the edge. Then you'd have the Hulk to deal with. Or you could take on the robots and their energy beams.

"Great choice," you think. "Getting smashed by the jolly green giant, or being vaporized by a pair of Rock 'Em Sock 'Em Robots."

What do you do?

IF YOU TRY TO RESCUE BANNER, GO TO CHAPTER 8, PAGE 94.

IF YOU TAKE ON THE ROBOTS, GO TO CHAPTER 9, PAGE 12.

39

CHAPTER 40

The cloaked figure of Doom looks like a child's action figure next to the towering bulk of the Hulk. The mad dictator lifts his steel mask toward the dull-witted green goliath. For once, you're happy at the thought of the Hulk smashing something. All you have to do is sit back and watch out for flying debris.

"TIN MAN!" the Hulk thunders. "Why did you trick Hulk? Hulk smash! Then Tin Man won't trick Hulk anymore!"

You can't help a little cheerleading. "Go get him, Hulk! Good luck, Doom!"

"You fool!" Doom says to you. "Doom fears no half-witted brute!"

"Hey, it's your funeral, Doc," you say, suddenly not so sure of yourself. Doom may be a dangerous madman, but he usually tells the truth when he brags about his schemes. You thought it was Banner he was after. What does he want the Hulk for?

"I . . . acquired Doctor Banner in order to do some tests," Doom continues, pacing back and forth right under the confused Hulk's nose. "It confirmed what I suspected. With astronium and a substance from the Hulk's blood, I can create a serum that will give me the Hulk's unmatched strength—and keep my superior intellect."

"Your superior wackiness, you mean." You deliver the line like you mean it, but inside you're feeling a little queasy. What if Doom can really do it? Time to stop this party before it gets out of hand. The Hulk is boiling with rage. Not only can't he understand most of what is being said, but just the mention of Banner's name is enough to send him into a fit.

"Banner!" he shouts. "Is he here to try to hurt Hulk?"

The Hulk lifts his giant fist above Doom's steel-masked head. Strangely, Doom seems completely unconcerned. In the next moment you see why.

"No, Hulk!"

It's a new voice. A woman's voice. You turn to see who could it belong to. When you see, you don't believe it. How could *she* be here?

You and the Hulk both stare at the young, pretty woman with dark brown hair standing in the doorway of what's left of the lab. She's wearing a light blue dress with a matching ribbon in her hair. Unless you're off your rocker, it's Betty Ross, Bruce Banner's wife and the one person in the world that the Hulk actually trusts. *How did she get here?* Things keep getting weirder and weirder.

"Betty!" the Hulk cries in joy. "Did Betty come to be with Hulk?"

"Yes, Hulk," Betty replies. She steps into the room, and your spider-sense begins tingling. Of course! It's not the real Betty Ross! It's got to be another of Doom's robots! Somehow Doom found out about Betty's power over the Hulk. Now he's going to use this robot of her to control the brute. This was Doom's plan all along!

"Great," you think. "Now that *I've* got it figured out, how do I explain it to pea brain?"

You don't have much time. Robot Betty walks to the giant green monster and takes his huge fist. Her hand and half her arm disappear in his grasp.

"Hulk," she says. "Spider-Man tricked you. Spider-Man wants to hurt you, not Doom."

"Bug-man?" Hulk repeats, struggling to understand. "But Tin Man said something about Banner. Hulk hates Banner."

"Never mind that," the Betty robot says soothingly. "Betty knows you don't like Banner. Betty will take care of it. But first you have to smash Spider-Man. Spider-Man wants to hurt Betty!"

"No!" you shout.

At the exact same time, the Hulk roars, *"No!"*

It's like shouting into a tornado. The Hulk drops the robot's hand and turns. He begins lumbering toward you.

GO TO CHAPTER 42, PAGE 16.

CHAPTER 22

Banner *does* seem more in control of himself than usual. Maybe he's learned how to keep from going over the edge. Anyway, you sure hope so. You take a deep breath and put your hand on his arm again, as gently as you can.

"Look—" you start to say.

Banner jerks his hand away again and by accident slams it into a sharp corner of the desk.

"Ow!" he shrieks. "I said, leave me alone! Don't you ever listen? Why is everyone persecuting me?"

"Dr. Banner . . ." you say, backing off. This is exactly what you were afraid of.

The scientist keeps ranting, his face growing redder every second. "First Doom, now you! Don't you think I know what's best? Why don't you all *leave me alone!*"

"This is it," you think as Banner flies into a rage. He's sweating, his breath is coming in short gasps. The signs are unmistakable. "Good-bye, Bruce, hello, Hulk."

For once, you're sorry you're right. A few seconds is all it takes. Banner's skin twists and changes, becoming green and thick like a rhinoceros hide. His figure swells and grows, his muscles bulge enormously, his face contorts and morphs into that of the incredible Hulk!

As though continuing Banner's fit, the Hulk brings his massive fist down on the heavy wooden desk, and it splinters into a thousand pieces.

"Leave Hulk alone!" he growls. He shakes his shaggy head as though waking from a deep sleep. He peers at you dully, trying to get his bearings.

"Bug-man?" he says, recognizing you. You wish he would find another name for you, but this is no time to quibble. Every guard in the place must have heard the crash of that desk being destroyed. You have to get the Hulk out of there. If you can.

"That's right, Hulk," you say softly. "It's, uh, good to see you again. Now, how about you and I go for a little walk?"

Trying to reason with the jolly green brute is like trying to reason with a tempermental five-year-old child who throws tantrums that have the force of a small earthquake. Still, you have to try.

"Come on, Hulk," you plead. "I'll even get you an ice cream cone. Or a nice big plate of beans."

The Hulk stares at you while his slow brain tries to digest what has happened.

"Leave Hulk alone, stupid bug-man," he growls. "Hulk doesn't like this place. Why is Hulk here? Did puny bug-man bring Hulk to this stupid place?"

"No, no," you say, trying to calm him. "I didn't *bring* you here. I want to get you out of here. How about being a nice Hulk and following the stupid bug-man?"

It seems as if an eternity goes by as the Hulk's feeble brain power tries to process this. Finally he seems to understand.

"Hulk go with bug-man?" he asks. "Away from here?"

"That's right!" you say. "You got it! Just come along and—"

Blam!

At that moment the door slams open and a platoon of Latverian guards run in. They are waving their automatic rifles and shouting at you and the Hulk.

"Stay where you are!" commands their leader.

The Hulk screams in anger. He turns to glare at you, his massive hands clenching into fists. "Bug-man lied! You try to trap Hulk!"

"No, Hulk!" you say. "It's not like th—"

"Hulk will smash stupid bug-man!" he shouts in a voice like the roar of a hurricane.

"So much for trying to calm him down," you think as the Hulk raises his massive green fist and throws a punch in your direction. You dodge it, and his arm goes straight *through* the thick stone wall of the mansion. The whole building shakes to its foundations.

You are caught between the Hulk and the guards, who have leveled their rifles and seem ready to shoot. It occurs to you, not for the first time, that maybe the best thing to do would be to get yourself out of there fast.

You could try to lure the Hulk away from the embassy by offering yourself as bait. But it might not work. And it would be pretty dangerous. Do you try it?

IF YOU TRY TO LURE THE HULK AWAY, GO TO CHAPTER 23, PAGE 71.

IF YOU TRY TO ESCAPE, GO TO CHAPTER 24, PAGE 142.

46

At that moment the door slams open and a platoon of Latverian guards run in.

CHAPTER 26

"Okay," you say, still feeling unsure. "If you think you can do it. But what if you turn into the Hulk? What happens then?"

Banner shakes his head. "It won't happen," he explains. He holds up a small bottle that he's kept concealed in his hand. "I've developed these new tranquilizers. They keep me from going into the transformation. At least they have so far."

No wonder Banner has been able to keep control through all these events. You nod in appreciation.

"Okay," you say, "I guess you know what you're doing. But we should have a signal, some way you can let me know if you're in trouble."

"*You're* the one in trouble," says a harsh, metallic voice.

It's Doctor Doom! He throws open the door to the bedroom and stalks in, followed by a group of black-suited Latverian guards. You tense to spring at him, but he moves too quickly, aiming his steel glove at Banner's

"You're *the one in trouble*," says a harsh, metallic voice.

head. You see an energy beam projector in the palm of Doom's gauntlet glowing hotly.

"Stop!" he warns. "If you want Banner to live!"

"You wouldn't," you say. "You need him for your astronium project."

"Yes, but if I can't use him, then no one else will," Doom replies. "Your choice, Spider-Man—surrender or be fated to remember that Banner's death was your fault."

Not wanting to risk Banner's life by attempting an escape, you surrender. Doom's men put extremely strong handcuffs around your wrists.

"Guards," orders Doom, "take them to the dungeon!"

Trailing after Doom, the guards lead you and Banner out of the room and down a stone staircase.

You're more than a little worried as they take you down into a very real dungeon. It's actually more of a laboratory, filled with computers and very sophisticated high-tech equipment. You allow the guards to strap you and Banner into form-fitting seats. You can't help but notice that the chairs are really very comfortable—for a prison.

"Hey, I've got to get me one of these for the TV room," you say. "Does it come with a recliner?"

"Let Spider-Man go, Doom," Banner

pleads as they strap him in, "and I'll go on helping you with your research!"

"You fool!" Doom shouts, slapping the scientist with his heavy glove. Dark red bruises appear on Banner's face. "It's not *you* I'm interested in," he cries, "but your blood!"

"My *blood?*" Banner's eyes fill with terror.

Suddenly you think you see Doom's real plan. He would never have killed Banner. You've been tricked again! You struggle against the bonds holding you down, but they don't budge.

"I couldn't understand why you wouldn't transform, Doctor Banner," Doom says, pacing in front of you. "Until you so nicely explained it just now." He holds up the bottle of tranquilizers and crushes it easily in his steel glove. "Thank you, Spider-Man, for getting me that important information."

"But why the Hulk?" Banner asks. "How can you possibly . . . ?"

"Silence!" Doom cries. Banner falls silent.

"I have done some studies," Doom continues in a calmer voice. "You want to use astronium to rid yourself of the Hulk. But I have something else in mind. If my calculations are correct—and they always are—then the right amount of astronium, reacting with a substance in your gamma-irradiated blood will produce a serum that will make me truly invincible. Do you understand the implications, Doctor? Thanks to your astronium, I have found a way to have all of the Hulk's power, combined with my mighty intellect! I will be truly superhuman!"

"No!" Banner screams in a mixture of anger and pain.

"No, Doctor Banner?" taunts Doom. "And what will you do to stop me—turn into your oafish, greenskinned alter-ego?" He laughs. "Then do so! Von Doom will control him as he controls all men!"

"No one can control the Hulk!" Banner shouts.

"No ordinary man, it is true," Doom responds. "But I am Doom. With the Hulk's limited intelligence, it will be child's play to make him do my bidding. He will help me collect the astronium I need for my plan!"

All this time, while Doom has been distracted by Banner, you've been working to get yourself free. Luckily, Doom neglected to remove your web-shooters. The shackles holding you are electronically controlled. If you can direct a stream of webbing into the locking mechanism, it might disrupt the signal that holds it shut. If you can just maneuver the shooter. You'll have only one shot before Doom notices your actions, so you'd better get it right.

"Fool!" Doom's steel mask is inches away from Banner's face. "Did you really think I needed your *brain*? When Victor von Doom possesses the most powerful scientific mind in the world?"

Doom slaps the scientist, harder this time. You hear Banner's breath coming in ragged gasps. You try to focus on getting free. You don't dare turn to look at what's happening, but you can guess. You've seen the signs before. If only you can get free before . . .

Craack!

You turn your head and see that Banner's chair has split into several small pieces. But then, Banner isn't there anymore, either—the transformation is complete. Standing next to you, looming over Doctor Doom, is the savage form of the incredible Hulk!

GO TO CHAPTER 27, PAGE 128.

CHAPTER 5

"If Banner turns into the Hulk," you realize, "there won't be any press conference left to report on. In fact, there may not be a building left to hold the press conference in."

You slip through the crowd of photographers who are gathered in front of the stage, snapping pictures madly. In the commotion, no one notices you step onto the stage and hurry through the doorway after Banner. There's no sign of him on the other side, so you step into a long hallway. It's only been a few seconds, he can't have gone very far.

There he is, down the corridor. He's pretty far away but even at this distance he still seems pretty angry. You're glad you decided to go after him.

You follow at a distance. What's best? Should you catch up with him and try to talk, or should you stay back and just watch him?

He's moving pretty quickly and you lose sight of him as he turns a corner up ahead. You run to catch up, your camera bag slapping at your side. As you turn the corner a few seconds later, you pull up short. Banner has just gone through a security door. There's an armed guard and some kind of machine that reads I.D. cards or fingerprints, or both. As Peter Parker, you can't follow him. Of course, it shouldn't be a problem for Spider-Man.

But that would mean changing into your costume and finding some way around the guard and then finding Banner again in the huge building. All of those things will take time and by then you're sure to miss the whole press conference.

You can still see Banner in the corridor

ahead, through the glass door. If you yell, he might hear you and come back. Then you could talk to him and still might make it back to the auditorium in time to take some pictures.

On the other hand, Banner is pretty steamed at the press. And you *are* working for the *Daily Bugle*. Being bugged by you just might push him even closer to becoming the Hulk. He's almost out of sight. What do you do?

IF YOU YELL FOR BANNER, GO TO CHAPTER 6, PAGE 65.

IF YOU CHANGE INTO YOUR SPIDER-MAN COSTUME, GO TO CHAPTER 7, PAGE 34.

CHAPTER 36

Wait a minute! Somewhere you heard someone talking about how to control astronium. Where was it? It seems like it was years ago, but it was really just yesterday, just as you arrived at GTC for the press conference. What was it those two scientists said?

That's right! They said a strong magnetic field can control astronium. You hope they were right, because that's the control you select.

For a few moments nothing seems to be happening. Then the computer voice starts up again.

"Chain reaction averted," it begins, and then it stops. The warning sign on the control screen disappears. The entire experiment shuts down. You did it!

Boom!

That sound behind you is the sound of the Hulk ripping open a wall like you might roll back a sardine can.

"Guess I'll just have to collect my medals later," you tell yourself as you turn and face the chaos behind you. You almost forgot—you still have the robots *and* the Hulk to deal with.

As if on cue, you hear a harsh, grating voice from the other side of what used to be a wall. Standing there in the rubble is Doctor Doom, his cruel steel face caught in a permanent sneer. He looks up at the looming figure of the Hulk, who has just ripped the last robot to pieces.

"Very good," the crazed genius declares. "Everything is going according to my plan!"

GO TO CHAPTER 40, PAGE 40.

CHAPTER 16

You can't resist. He's like a sitting duck down there. You'll never have a chance like this again. Almost joyfully you push off from your perch on the wall and fly through space, straight down toward the waiting Doom. And then, at the last moment, your spider-sense goes off like a siren in your head!

Kaboom!

Doctor Doom explodes in a fireball of orange and blue flames. You're thrown sideways, crashing with tremendous impact into the hard paving stones of the courtyard. Searing pain in your legs tells you that you're hurt—hurt bad.

And then a door opens in the mansion and a tall, green-cloaked figure strides into the growing darkness. His steel gauntlets gleam in the dull light and instead of a face he has a cruel-looking steel mask.

It wasn't the real Doom you tried to attack, you realize, but a robot decoy. Standing before you is the true Doom and he was waiting for you. It was all a trap.

The sound of heavy boots on the paving

stones rings in your ears. You are surrounded by a platoon of Doom's heavily-armed Latverian guards.

"Now, Doomsy," you manage to croak through the pain, "is this any way to welcome an old pal?"

Doom's harsh voice cuts you off. "Save what passes for your wit, Spider-Man. You have precious little of it as it is. At long last you have fallen into my clutches. I promise you will never escape them again! Never!"

Doom's harsh laugh echoes in the closing night. For once you think he may be right. There's no way you can get out now.

THE END

CHAPTER 44

You realize that if *you* attack "Betty" it will just make the Hulk angrier.

But, what if someone *else* attacks her?

The Hulk reappears in the room, waving a twenty-foot steel girder at you like a baseball bat.

"Betty is Hulk's friend! Bug-man leave Betty alone!"

The Hulk storms toward you, swinging the

Doctor Doom explodes in a fireball of orange and blue flames.

girder. You know that if you make one false move, you'll be swatted like a fly. You leap backward. The Hulk charges past the spot you were just standing and keeps going.

"That guy needs to have his brakes checked," you think. Meanwhile you're swinging toward Doctor Doom. The Latverian madman has been watching the whole time. He's not exactly caught off-guard as you swing toward him on a line of webbing, but then you want him to see you coming.

"Hey Doom!" you shout. "Heads up!"

Doom lifts his gauntlets and lets loose with a blast of his energy cannon. But you were expecting that. You flip forward just in time and the beam shoots past without hitting you. You bounce forward, again acting like you're trying to get to Doom. You have to be careful because the Hulk has turned around again. He's coming back in your direction like a freight train. But all you need is a few more seconds.

"What's the matter, Doom?" you taunt as you swing toward the cloaked figure. "You need ol' greenie to protect you?"

"Doom can handle you or any other cretin who gets in his way!" he shouts, firing another blast. You turn as it rockets past.

"Better watch out Doom," you cry. "You're beginning to talk like our green-skinned pal."

The Hulk leaps for you. This is it. You

swing around on a web-line. The Hulk misses. Doom is firing at you with both gauntlets now. You trail off to the side. One, two, three . . . bingo!

The last blast from Doom hits the Betty robot! Bits of wire, transistors, computer chips and other electronic parts go spraying across the room. "Betty" collapses like a puppet whose strings have been cut.

The Hulk's wail is like the roaring wind.

"Betty!"

The rage vanishes from his face and is replaced by a look of total loss and grief. For a moment you feel sorry for the poor lug. The green behemoth rushes to the remains of his friend and picks up pieces the melted plastic and wiring. The sadness fades and becomes pained confusion. Neither you nor Doom have moved.

"This not Betty?" the Hulk moans. "Not Hulk's friend? Hulk's head hurts . . ."

The saucer-sized eyes suddenly bulge with anger again.

"Tin Man did this! You make Betty not Betty! Then you kill her!"

"Hulk!" Doom says, trying to command the brute. "Listen to me!"

"No!" the Hulk screams. "You listen! Listen to this!"

And faster than you've ever seen him move, the mighty Hulk pounces on the steel-masked madman. Before you have time to think, he rips off Doom's head. Then he stops. He peers at Doom's body. Then he looks at you.

"This not real Tin Man," the Hulk says wonderingly. "Hulk not understand. Bug-man, you understand?"

You think, "Good question."

Cautiously, you edge closer to the Hulk. The great green brute holds Doom's body carelessly. The first glance of the wires sticking out of its neck and you realize you've been tricked again. That isn't Doom. It's another robot, a Doombot.

"It's a robot," you say to the still confused Hulk.

He looks at the shattered figure in his hand and tosses it aside with contempt.

"Not real Betty!" he says. "Not real Tin Man. Are you real Bug-man?"

"Yes!" you say as strongly as you can. You're afraid that the Hulk might want to take a look at your insides also. He scratches his massive head.

"Hulk wants to smash," he says, almost sadly. "But Hulk can't remember why. Bug-man remember?"

"Nope," you answer, trying to sound cheerful. "It must have been something you ate."

"You should smash him because he is an interfering pest!"

You've heard that voice before. In fact, you

heard it last just a few seconds ago. It belongs to Doctor Doom!

The entire roof of the lab is gone and most of the walls have been leveled. You and the Hulk turn and see a green-cloaked, steel-masked figure floating out of the sky. He's powered by a jet pack. He lands not far away.

"You've gotten in my way one too many times," he begins. "But you won't stop me this time!"

"I think I already have," you boast.

"You fool!" Doom cries. "A pitiful mind like yours is no match for my genius. I am far from defeated!"

"You're too late, Doom!" you respond. "You can forget about using the Hulk."

"I may not be able to control the Hulk," Doom counters. "But I can still control the astronium!"

"Maybe," you say. "But you're forgetting one little thing. The Hulk knows you tricked him. Right, Hulk?"

"Stupid bug-man is right!" the Hulk cries. "Tin Man tricked to Hulk with fake Betty! Hulk wants to see real Betty! What did Tin Man do with real Betty?"

"Go get him, Hulk!" you urge.

The Hulk doesn't need much encouragement. With a roar, he charges toward Doom.

"Hulk smash!" he thunders.

"Yes," says another voice. "But whom will you smash?"

The Hulk skids to a halt and shouts in frustration. Behind you, another Doom is floating down out of the sky. He's identical to the first.

"It's another robot!" you shout, as the Hulk looks back and forth with mounting anger.

"Hulk hates Tin Man! Hulk hates fake Tin Man—Hulk will smash both!"

The green gargantua turns and charges back. You step aside as he thunders past you, headed for the new Doom.

"Yes, but what about me?" calls yet another familiar voice.

A *third* Doom has appeared, stepping through the wreckage. The Hulk sees that one and whips around. He stamps his feet in anger and the ground buckles. You're almost thrown off-balance.

"Three Tin Men!" he roars. "Hulk will smash you all!"

"But first you'll have to catch me!" say all three Dooms at once. They turn and run off in different directions. One takes off into the air and seems to be flying away from the General Techtronics complex. One runs off through the rubble toward a nearby research building. The third runs through the wreckage toward Bruce Banner's lab.

"Bug-man!" the Hulk shouts. "Tin Man is getting away. Hulk will smash—but which one? Bug Man tell Hulk!"

Bug-man would like to tell Hulk, you think, only bug-man isn't too sure himself. One of those is probably the real Doom, but which one? The Hulk is waiting for an answer, and you know he's not very patient. What will you do?

IF YOU CHASE THE DOOM WHO IS FLYING AWAY, GO TO CHAPTER 45, PAGE 117.

IF YOU CHASE THE DOOM WHO IS RUNNING TOWARD BRUCE BANNER'S LAB, GO TO CHAPTER 46, PAGE 87.

IF YOU CHASE THE DOOM RUNNING TO A NEARBY BUILDING, GO TO CHAPTER 47, PAGE 26.

CHAPTER 6

"Dr. Banner!"

You shout as loudly as you can, trying not to startle him. It doesn't come out exactly the way you'd hoped. The scientist halts in mid-stride and turns to peer at you, bristling with anger.

"No photographers allowed back here,"

the guard starts to warn you, but Banner interrupts him.

"Can't you reporters leave me alone!" he shouts and rushes toward you.

This is not working out at all the way you wanted. Instead of calming Banner down, you're getting him even more agitated.

"Sorry!" you say as you back away. You smile as reassuringly as you can. "I didn't mean to bug you. I . . . I . . ."

"I know what you wanted!" Banner shouts, his eyes glaring. "You wanted to persecute me! But . . ."

Somehow the scientist catches himself. You see the strain on his face ease a little and he takes a deep breath.

"I'm not going to let you people drive me over the edge," he says, almost to himself. He straightens himself and seems to calm down. "If you want to talk to me," he says evenly, "make an appointment through the GTC press office."

"Sure. Okay. No problem," you nod, smiling politely.

You back up some more and watch as Banner turns and walks down the corridor again, this time in a nice, steady walk. Instead of kicking the door open, he pushes it with his hand, almost gently. You see his back disappear through the doorway. Only then do you start breathing again.

"Some temper, huh?" you say to the security guard, who gives you a knowing look of agreement.

You turn and start walking quickly in the direction of the auditorium. With any luck, you think, Langkowski will still be talking.

"I bet he hasn't even started the demonstration," you say to yourself, feeling downright happy. But your feeling of elation disappears in the next instant, as your early warning spider-sense goes haywire.

Boom!

A thundering explosion rocks the entire GTC complex. The floor under your feet sways for a moment. Then a thick cloud of black smoke shoots into the hallway. It's coming from the auditorium! Something went wrong with the demonstration! And that place was packed with people.

You don't have time to find a good hiding place to change into your Spider-Man costume, so you jump to the ceiling and hang upside down while you change, hoping that no one spots you in the few seconds it takes. A moment later you drop to the floor and run toward the accident with all your might.

Dazed and bleeding survivors are stumbling out of the room, choking on the thick smoke. But your spider-sense is calm. Any danger that was here is now gone. That means the worst is over, you think, as you plunge through the smoke and into the auditorium.

Worst is the right word. Just a few minutes

earlier the room was a spotless, gleaming mix of polished wood and high-tech equipment. Now it's a charred, twisted wreck. Injured scientists and reporters are lying unconscious, their bodies tossed about like dolls.

"The R.A.D.," you think. "It must have exploded."

You shoot a web-line toward the ceiling and swing your way over toward the stage. But even as you do, you can see that it's the least damaged place in the hall. Langkowski is lying on the wooden floor, unconscious. Otherwise he seems unhurt. But the spot where the R.A.D. machine stood is now empty.

And then, as the smoke clears you see the source of the explosion. There's a gaping hole in the outside wall of the auditorium. It's clear from the blast marks that someone placed a charge outside and blew the wall in. You swing over to the jagged opening.

The bright sunlight blinds you for an instant, and then you see, above the rooftops, a group of jet-powered robots. Their chrome bodies are dwindling in the distance even as you catch sight of them. They're too far off for you to catch up to. But they're not too far away for you to recognize what they're carrying—the R.A.D. machine.

"Someone stole the machine—and the astronium!" you realize as you stand there helplessly. "Whoever did it didn't care how many people got hurt, either."

Your heart sinks as you realize that if you had only stayed at the press conference like you were supposed to, you would have been there when the attack occurred.

"I could have stopped them," you think. "Or at least saved some of these people from getting hurt."

As you stand there, mentally kicking yourself, a tiny sound edges into your consciousness. You recognize it immediately. A photographer, already recovered from the blast, is snapping pictures.

"Great!" you moan inwardly. "Not only did I let the astronium get stolen, but now I don't even have any photos for Jameson. He's going to kill me!"

THE END

CHAPTER 10

"I'm not Banner's nursemaid," you grumble. "Besides, he seems to have himself under control, for once. And I have a job to do, getting pictures for that ol' skinflint Jameson."

You shake off thoughts of Banner and turn your attention once more to Dr. Langkowski and the astronium-powered R.A.D. machine.

You squeeze off a picture as Langkowski explains the machine's operation. You doubt that most of the press can follow it. Even with your scientific training some of it is difficult to follow. But the gist of the whole thing is that through the use of astronium, the R.A.D. can make deadly radioactive material safe.

"If it works," you add mentally.

As the scientist drones on, you notice that Bruce Banner has quietly returned to the room, although he stays at the rear of the stage where few people can notice him.

"I was right—for once," you congratulate yourself. "He calmed down all on his lonesome."

It seems that you might actually be able to complete an assignment for the *Bugle*. And better yet, you might actually get paid. You're feeling awfully good about things when your spider-sense goes off like a fire alarm.

You brace yourself for—what? An explosion? A blow to the head? Usually your spider-sense gives you a split-second warning of immediate danger, but this seems more general. Something is about to go wrong. Langkowski has his hands on the R.A.D. control panel. Could it be the device? Is there something wrong with it? Has it been sabotaged?

You cringe as Langkowski proceeds calmly

with the demonstration. You could jump on stage and stop him. But how would you explain it? Besides, what if you have to go into Spidey-mode? Maybe you'd better duck out and change into your web-slinging outfit.

What do you do?

IF YOU RUN AND CHANGE INTO SPIDER-
MAN, GO TO CHAPTER 11, PAGE 91.

IF YOU STAY AND STOP THE
DEMONSTRATION, GO TO CHAPTER 14,
PAGE 82.

CHAPTER 23

The Hulk might follow you out of there, if you can just get him mad enough at you. And *that* shouldn't be a problem.

"Hey Greenie!" you say. "You've got something in your eye!" You fire a glob of webbing, covering his face with the gray strands.

The Hulk growls and thunders toward you as he pulls off the webbing. But at the same time, the Latverian guards open fire! They're aiming at you, but the Hulk's broad green back serves as a shield. The bullets bounce off him and ricochet around the room.

"*Arrgh!*" Stupid men try to hurt Hulk with their guns. Now Hulk will smash!"

And smash he does. Boulder-size fragments go flying past you at dizzying speed. The balcony, the wall, the entire side of the mansion gives way and collapses to the ground.

You wake up in great pain, pinned to the earth by tons of stone and steel. The entire wing of the embassy lies in ruins around you. There's no sign of the Hulk. But though there's no Hulk, there are plenty of Latverian guards. They ring you, guns at the ready. In the center of the ring stands Doctor Doom.

"My plans ruined!" he cries shaking his metal fist at you. "My embassy destroyed! Because of you! This is the last time you will meddle in my plans, I promise you. You've ruined my mansion, but you will never leave it . . . alive!"

THE END

CHAPTER 35

Y ou can't leave the experiment. If it blows up, hundreds of people could be killed. You'll just have to take your chances with the Hulk. And it's a good thing you decided to let him transform, you think. Because he's already doing it.

In a matter of seconds, the small, wounded Bruce Banner morphs and grows until he's the massive, muscle-bound figure of the Hulk. His wound closes up and heals. His skin turns a dark green. His brow bulges, his hair transforms into a shaggy mane. He towers above the computer console and stares at it dully with his great, vacant eyes.

"Where is Hulk now? What is this television?"

You're about to break the news to him. Not only isn't it TV but there's isn't even a remote. But your spider-sense tells you it's time to jump—fast!

You leap straight up and the blast from the Doombots' sonic cannons flows past and hits the Hulk square in the back. It doesn't even buckle his knees. But it *does* get his attention.

You cling to the ceiling as the green brute turns and sees the two robots.

"Where did Tin Men come from?" he grunts. "Why do stupid Tin Men try to hurt Hulk? Don't Tin Men know no one can hurt Hulk? Hulk will hurt *them!*"

Great! For once things are breaking your way. The Hulk lumbers into the path of the oncoming robots. They separate and try to take the Hulk from both sides. But you don't have time to worry about the Hulk.

"Someone should worry about the robots instead," you tell yourself. "They're the ones facing the Hulkster."

You drop to the floor in front of the computer screen and turn your back to the battle. A quick glance at the readouts tell you that the experiment is not going as planned. It's just as Banner feared. Something has shifted the balance of the astronium.

As you watch, a red warning sign appears on the screen. A robotic voice says from within the computer, "Warning. Chain reaction probable. Abort!"

"Hulk smash Tin Men. Then maybe Tin Men will leave Hulk alone!"

A very large piece of furniture goes flying past you and splinters against the Plexiglas wall that separates you from the experiment. You hear the sound of small missiles being fired. But that's not what's making you sweat. Even though he doesn't know it, the Hulk is

"Hulk smash Tin Men. Then maybe Tin Men will leave Hulk alone!"

covering your back. And he can take a lot of punishment.

What's making you sweat is the thought of what will happen if you don't follow the computer's advice and shut down the experiment. The whole General Techtronics complex will blow sky high. Only how do you do it?

You select a new screen and see a diagram of the experiment. You can see quite clearly that there are two controls built into the program. One reverses the direction of the process. The other turns on a powerful magnetic field. Which is the right one to press?

"Chain reaction about to start!" says the computer's voice.

ACTIVATE THE MAGNETIC FIELD AND
GO TO CHAPTER 36, PAGE 55.

PUT THE EXPERIMENT INTO REVERSE
AND GO TO CHAPTER 37, PAGE 115.

CHAPTER 41

There's really only one place to go—back to General Techtronics. There's a missing piece of information. Why did Doom kidnap Banner? What is his *real* plan? Somewhere in Banner's notes or in his computer files there might be some clue. Besides, it's too late to catch *The Tonight Show* on television.

As you web-sling over the Manhattan rooftops, you try to review what you know about astronium and Banner's research. Unfortunately, it's not that much. It would help if you knew what you were looking for. Still, a little poking around might turn something up.

The General Techtronics complex is still in an uproar over Doom's robot attack. The place is ringed by police, security guards and dozens of reporters. For a minute you think of changing back to your Peter Parker clothes and slipping in as a member of the press.

"Too much trouble," you decide. Especially when all you have to do is aim your last web-swing so it's high enough to send you flying over the spotlights. You drop easily to the roof of the research building.

After that, it's a piece of cake to slip past

the GTC security barriers and into Banner's laboratory. Getting into his computer files isn't.

"That guy really *is* smart," you think after your tenth try at breaking his password.

You try a different approach, going through his written notes, his books, the papers on his desk, anything that looks like it might have a clue. You're still at it hours later, as dawn breaks over the GTC complex. You're feeling beat and you know your brain isn't working at top speed anymore. Still you keep at it, reading the notes over and over, bleary-eyed.

Then you think you've found something. Banner was working on a way to neutralize the used astronium so it couldn't be used for weapons. That sounds like something Bruce Banner would do, but it doesn't sound like something Doctor Doom would want.

In fact, it's something Doom would want to stop. If Doom had an astronium-based weapon, then he would want to stop Banner from completing his experiments. That would explain why the mad Latverian kidnapped the scientist. This could be what you're looking for. Only now that you've found it, what do you do with it? You stand up and walk to the window. It's light outside now. Maybe you should go home, have some breakfast, catch some shut eye. Maybe even say "Hi" to that gorgeous wife of yours, Mary Jane. It sounds pretty inviting. You're just about to give in to it, when . . .

Boom!

A shudder like a minor earthquake shakes the entire building. You're thrown off-balance. As you recover, the building shakes again. Something is rattling it around like a child's toy. And you're pretty sure you know what that something is—the incredible Hulk!

A green fist the size of a pumpkin smashes through the thick steel plates of the lab door. The door is torn from its hinges. In through the jagged hole walks, not the Hulk, but Doctor Doom!

The evil madman strides in like he owns the place. His green cloak brushes the floor. His weird steel mask glares at you. He points a gleaming steel glove at you, but instead of launching an energy blast, he only speaks.

"Surrender, Spider-Man!"

"Doom, you sound more and more like the Wicked Witch of the West," you quip. At the same time, your whole being is alert. Something weird is going on. Banner has transformed into the Hulk, but where is the big green brute?

"You don't have a chance," Doom insists.

"Come on, Doom," you reply. "Aren't you being a little cocky?"

"Not at all," he answers. His voice is like two metal files rasping against each other. "Hulk? Would you come in here?"

Now you see something that astonishes you more than anything you can remember. The incredible Hulk, all thousand pounds of him, enters through the broken doorway. And he's as docile as a lamb. The rippling green muscles, the awesome power, is completely under the control of Doctor Doom.

You can't help yourself. "How . . ." you begin to stammer. Then you see the answer to your question. Right behind the Hulk is a smaller figure. A pretty young woman, wearing a blue dress. It's Betty Ross, Bruce Banner's wife. She's the only human being the Hulk really trusts. What is she doing here?

Then it hits you—it's not the real Betty Ross! It's another one of Doom's robots. Somehow Doom found out about the Hulk's feelings for Betty. The crazed Latverian leader is using the robot to control the Hulk.

The Betty robot stares up at the Hulk with admiring eyes. The Hulk looks down at her with an expression you've never seen before on that brutish green face. It's friendship— perhaps even love. You stand there, dumbstruck. But Doom is gloating.

"You see, you buffoon," Doom says. "Doom is prepared for every situation. With astronium and a substance taken from the Hulk's blood, I can produce a serum that will give me his great strength—without losing my immense intellect. Then I will be truly unstoppable!"

Doom laughs. The thought chills you to the marrow. Doctor Doom, with his evil genius intact and with the Hulk's unstoppable power? It's a truly frightening thought. Doom hasn't stopped bragging.

"And there's an extra benefit to my plan. Perhaps even a dull-witted creature like yourself may have guessed it. My new green friend is not only very good at collecting astronium, he's also excellent at getting rid of anyone who stands in my way. Like yourself!"

Up till now the Hulk has been ignoring everything around him. He hasn't really heard a word that Doom has said. Even if he *had* heard it, you doubt he would have understood any of it. But now the Betty Ross robot steps forward and speaks for the first time.

"Hulk," she says, in a soft, melodious voice. "Do you see Spider-Man?"

The Hulk looks at you curiously.

"Hulk sees bug-man," he says.

"Spider-Man wants to hurt me," the robot says. "He wants to hurt Betty. You won't let him hurt me, will you?"

GO TO CHAPTER 42, PAGE 16.

CHAPTER 14

"I've got to move—now!" you realize.

There's no time to change into your Spider-Man duds. You drop your camera and in spite of everything, you groan inwardly as you hear a breaking noise. But there isn't the time to worry about photographic equipment. As the audience gasps in shock, you jump onstage and throw yourself in a full body block across Dr. Langkowski and Bruce Banner, knocking them both to the floor.

"What?" Banner shouts, turning red. "Who are—"

His next words are drowned completely by the sound of a massive explosion that rips open the wall of the auditorium. Large chunks of brick and steel fly through the air, right past the spot where moments ago the two scientists were standing.

The room is in chaos. Some people are screaming, others are standing in shock. You lift your head and try to untangle yourself from Dr. Langkowski. Something is coming in through the hole, though you can't quite make it out through the smoke and dust.

The room is in chaos.

Whatever it is, you realize that you can't do much about it as Peter Parker. You get to your knees and look for a spot to change. As you do a bright blue beam of light strikes you. You have a feeling like the end of a telephone pole has struck you in the temple. Then everything goes black.

You wake up out of a deep, peaceful sleep to find yourself still on the stage, surrounded by faces. And most of them belong to policemen.

"He's the one," someone is saying. "He knew the blast was going to happen. He rushed the stage right before it hit. He must be part of the gang that kidnapped Bruce Banner."

Kidnapped Bruce Banner? You try to open your mouth to protest but all that comes out are some garbled sounds.

"Take him away," says one of the police officers. "This photographer has got some questions to answer."

The words keep echoing in your brain. "Kidnapped Bruce Banner." But who? And why? And how can they blame you?

With a sinking heart you realize that not only did you fail to protect Banner, you're in trouble with the police. And not only are you in trouble with the police, but you broke your camera! That means no pictures for J. Jonah Jameson!

As they load you into the ambulance, all you can think is, "I've got to get out of the super hero business."

THE END

CHAPTER 48

"**H**ey, Doc! Up here!"

It's an evening one week later. You're back at General Techtronics. Slowly, the construction crews are rebuilding the damaged buildings. You've been hanging out—hanging on the side of a building, waiting to talk to Bruce Banner.

The events of the past seven days have been a dream come true for *Daily Bugle* publisher J. Jonah Jameson: The Hulk went on a rampage and destroyed some real estate. A major disaster that could have wiped out the East Coast was averted. The United Nations learned of Doctor Doom's plans to take over the world and threw him out of the United States. The Latverian Embassy was closed and its staff sent home. Best of all, Spider-Man was involved, so Jonah has someone to blame for the whole mess.

You drop down to the pavement to talk to Banner.

"How's it going?" you ask. "Things settling down?"

Banner breaks into a broad smile.

"Everything is fine," he says, "thanks to you. I've managed to piece together what happened with Doctor Doom. I know what the Hulk did, and how close Doom got to getting his hands on the astronium."

"That's what I wanted to talk—" you begin to say, but Banner cuts you off.

"You don't need to ask, Spider-Man," he says. "I've already destroyed all the astronium, *and* my notes on the process. The GTC Board of Directors was pretty unhappy, but I convinced them the world just isn't ready for something so dangerous."

"You did the right thing, Doc," you say. "I know it must have been hard for you to do it. You were kind of hoping that astronium would lead to a cure for you."

"Yes, I was," Banner says with a sigh. "But better that I should continue living with the spectre of the Hulk looming over me than to put the entire world at risk with astronium. I'll just have to keep on looking for a cure."

You and Banner shake hands.

"Thanks again, Spider-Man," says Banner. "I appreciate all your help."

"Hey, I couldn't have stopped Doom without you, Doc," you say. "Or your big, green alter-ego."

Banner's face lights up with a smile. "The

Hulk *did* do some good, didn't he?" He turns and heads back toward his laboratory. "Take care, Spider-Man," he says.

"You too, Doc," you answer as he walks into the building. "And good luck."

THE END

CHAPTER 46

"The astronium is here, in this building," you realize. "Doom is going to Banner's lab to find the combination to the vault where the astronium is kept."

"Which one, bug-man?" the Hulk repeats.

"That one!" you shout, pointing through the shattered doorway. You take off at a run, but the Hulk barrels past you. It's like racing a freight train. But in the hall beyond there's no sign of Doom. The green behemoth glances about angrily.

"Which way did Tin Man go?" the Hulk demands.

"Follow me!" you say.

You run toward Banner's office, the Hulk almost trampling you in his excitement. His enormous feet slam into the floor like jackhammers.

You're so busy avoiding getting squashed that you almost don't realize that your spider-sense is tingling like mad. You dodge just in time as an energy blast takes away part of the wall behind you.

"Give up, Doom!" you cry at the cloaked figure up ahead.

"You are the one who will surrender!" Doom shouts back.

You see Doom leveling one of his gauntlets at you.

"Hulk, watch out!" you shout as you dive for cover.

"Hulk is not afraid of stupid light," the behemoth growls.

The blast catches the Hulk in the chest. It doesn't even sting him.

Doom has fled, so you pick yourself off the wall and run after him. The Hulk pounds after you and sometimes kicks through a wall when it gets in his way. With every turn of the hallway you brace yourself for another attack by Doom. But nothing happens.

Less than a minute later you see the door to Banner's office. It's wide open and Doom is inside, bending over the computer screen, punching keys on the keyboard.

The Latverian madman seems completely absorbed in what he's doing. If you can get in there fast enough, before he has time to react, you might be able to catch him off-guard. The Hulk is lumbering behind you.

Any moment the noise he's making will alert Doom to your presence. It's now or never.

You throw your weight into the swing as you go through the doorway. Your feet are aimed straight for Doom's back. Then your spider-sense clicks in. You hurried, trying to beat the Hulk and now it's too late. It's a trap! It's . . .

Bam!

Something strikes you in the head but you don't feel any pain, just a numbing impact. You roll forward, hitting the ground, hard. You try to shake it off, get to your feet, but something is binding your arms and legs. You look down and see steel cables have wrapped themselves around you.

"Meddling arachnid!"

It's Doom's voice. But it's coming from behind you. You twist your head and there he is. The real Doom was waiting for you, setting a trap. The Doom at the desk is a fake, a robot.

"You fool!" the real Doom gloats. "I knew you would follow me here. I knew you would try to guard the codes for the astronium. It was the perfect place for a trap. Now you're finished!"

Not yet. You feel a shuddering in the floor. It can only mean one thing. Either there's a volcano erupting under Manhattan, or the Hulk has finally found the office. The Hulk can get you out of this!

"Hulk smash!"

You've never been happier to hear that voice. The green giant bursts into the small room.

"Hulk!" you shout. "Get Doom. I mean, get Tin Man!"

"Hulk smash Tin Man!" he shouts.

"Yes, Hulk, try to smash me!" says Doom. Only it's not the real Doom, it's the robot. It jumps through the window and flies away, propelled by jets on its steel boots.

"Don't worry, bug-man!" the Hulk cries. "Hulk will catch him!"

"No!" you scream. "It's the wrong . . ."

But it's too late. The last thing you see is the Hulk jumping clear through the wall, following the Doombot.

You don't know how much time has gone by when you finally wake up. But you can tell you're back at Doom's mansion. You're strapped to a table and there's a tube in your arm. Incredibly, the Hulk is lying on a platform next to you, unconscious. And there's a tube in his arm, also.

"What's happening?" you ask.

The steel-masked face of Doctor Doom appears.

"Things have worked out better than I thought," he says. "It seems that I can go ahead with my experiment as planned. But first I'm going to test it on you. "

"You mean—" you gasp.

"Yes," Doom laughs. "You are about to gain some of the Hulk's qualities. Not his strength of course. I'll make sure of that. But I think I can guarantee you green skin. And of course his wonderful temper and intellect."

"No!" you shout, straining at your bonds. But it's too late for you.

THE END

CHAPTER 11

Your spider-sense tingles even stronger.

"Something *baaaad* is about to happen," you tell yourself, as you slip to the back of the auditorium. "And whatever it is, I'll handle it a lot better as Spider-Man."

You rush out of the room, and into the deserted lobby. Quickly you climb a wall and hang upside down as you change into your costume. Only a handful of seconds have gone by as you fall lightly to the ground and race back to the door. You fling it open and get hit full in the face with the force of an explosive shock wave.

Baaam!

A huge section of the auditorium wall has been blown in, sending debris flying across the audience. Screams of wounded and frightened people fill the air and already you're in danger of being trampled as a panic-stricken mob starts to fight its way to the exits. You shoot a web-line to the ceiling and hoist yourself out of the way of the onrushing crowd.

Your new perch gives you a good vantage point, but what you see isn't pretty. Three giant, humanoid robots have climbed in through the hole in the wall and are making their way toward the stage. Each is studded with sensors and nasty-looking weaponry.

"They're after the R.A.D. machine," you realize. "And the astronium. Not if this little spider can help it."

The robots are picking their way over the seats and sprawled bodies. They don't move very quickly, but nothing seems to faze them. As you watch, a security guard wades through the crowd, draws his revolver and aims it at the nearest robot.

"Stop!" you try to warn him as you swing down. It all happens too quickly. You're still in mid-swing when a beam of energy shoots out of one of the robot's "eyes" and strikes the guard full in the chest. He crumples to the ground like a limp doll. The robot moves on toward the stage, the guard already forgotten.

You drop quickly to the side of the fallen man. A fast check tells you he's alive, just stunned.

"Take it easy, fella," you say reassuringly. "Let your friendly neighborhood Spider-Man handle these guys."

You glance up and see that the first robot

has already climbed onto the stage. Langkowski lies unconscious in front of the R.A.D. machine. But over his fallen body and directly in the robots' path stands a very small-looking Bruce Banner. You figure he must have come running back to the auditorium at the sound of the robots breaking in.

"The doc's a brave guy, but he's definitely out of his league here," you think as you hurtle over the seats toward the stage. "There's no way he can stop those robots from grabbing the R.A.D.—unless he becomes the Hulk."

You're not sure which would be worse— fighting off the three robots or having the Hulk around. You are sure you don't want to find out. You're going to have to get Banner and Langkowski out of there.

But if you grab Banner and Langkowski, the robots are sure to grab the R.A.D. You're going to have to make a choice.

IF YOU GRAB BANNER, GO TO CHAPTER 13, PAGE 105.

IF YOU GRAB THE R.A.D. GO TO CHAPTER 12, PAGE 103.

CHAPTER 8

The robots still seem frozen in place. You do a back handspring and come up next to Banner.

"Come on, Doc," you urge. "You don't really believe I'd do all this just to bug you. Not when I could just hit you with a slew of my worst jokes."

"I don't know what your game is, Spider-Man," Banner spits at you. "And I don't care."

"Look!" you shout. "Those recycled tin heaps were sent here by some baddie. They're after you. That means you have to get out of here!"

"No!" Banner shouts. "*You* have to get out of here! I can take care of myself."

There's no use arguing with him. You'll just have to carry him to safety in spite of himself. As gently as you can, you reach out and grab his arm. Just as you do, he hits one more button on the keyboard.

"Why'd you do that?" he screams. He tries to swat your hand away, but of course you're too strong for him. He struggles to get free. This is all wrong. Your spider-sense starts buzzing even stronger. Something bad is going to happen—now. Only what, you wonder? The robots will wake up? Banner will become the Hulk?

You have your answer in the next few seconds.

First the air immediately around you begins to crackle and buzz. You can sense some sort of energy field, only it's not coming from the robots. It's something that Banner set off with his computer. You realize suddenly that it's a force field. He activated it to protect himself from the robots.

As if on cue, the robots choose that moment to spring to life. They step forward, reaching out their hands. There's a loud explosion as they are repelled backward by the force field.

"Nice job, Doc," you say approvingly, turning to him. Only Banner is no longer there. You find yourself holding the massive, muscled, very green arm of the Hulk! Banner has snapped under the pressure.

The Hulk towers above you, a look of puzzlement covering his craggy green features.

"Where is Hulk?" he thunders. "What is that noise? Why is bug-man holding Hulk?"

Needless to say, you let go of his arm immediately.

"Now, Greenie," you say, almost in a whisper. "Let's not jump to conclusions."

"Jump?" the Hulk stares at you with distaste. "Hulk *will* jump. Hulk will jump far away from puny bug-man!"

"Wait," you start to explain. "That was only a figure of speech—"

It's too late. The Hulk has already crouched and sprung up with tremendous force, his fist aimed at the ceiling, like a living battering ram. And he probably would break through, if Bruce Banner hadn't switched on that force field. Because the field is not only strong enough to keep robots out. It can also keep the Hulk *in*.

As soon as the Hulk's hand touches the energy field, it crackles and sparks fly.

"YEOW!!" The Hulk screams in pain and falls, his feet driving straight through the solid floor. With an ear-splitting crash, the entire room disappears into the crater the Hulk has split open. You, the Hulk, and several tons of office furniture and equipment tumble to the basement below.

The Hulk lifts himself out of the wreckage. Of course, he isn't hurt at all. You, on the other hand, can barely breathe because of the desk, file cabinets and steel girders that lie across your aching back.

"Bug-man hurt Hulk!" the green behemoth shouts. His voice alone shakes loose a few more beams from the floor above you.

You consider trying to reason with him as he towers over you. But reasoning has never been the Hulk's strong point. You struggle to get out of the wreckage but you can't move. Helplessly, you watch the Hulk move closer.

"Bug-man hurt Hulk," he repeats, as if you didn't hear him the first time. "Now Hulk will hurt bug-man!"

At that moment the pain becomes too much and you black out. For a long time your mind floats in a sea of darkness. Then slowly, slowly, you begin to wake up. When you do, the Hulk is gone. In fact the whole GTC complex is gone.

You're now in some sort of dark chamber. You realize that you've been strapped down on a table, your arms and legs secured with thick metal bands. And standing before you is Doctor Doom, the brilliantly evil ruler of Latveria and your sworn enemy.

"Good morning, Spider-Man," he laughs in his harsh voice. "I must admit when I sent my robots to capture Bruce Banner, I never thought I'd wind up with you instead. How lucky for me. How very unlucky for you!"

"Great!" you think, as your head swims with pain. "I'm the catch of the day! And Doc Doom is going to have me on a platter!"

THE END

CHAPTER 31

"**D**oom is up to something—but what?" You and Banner are back at General Techtronics, in the most secure wing of the complex. You tried to convince Banner to go somewhere else, to hide out until you figured out what Doom was up to, but the scientist stubbornly refused. So you've spent the night standing watch over him. You've already called the Fantastic Four for help, but they're out of town.

In the background you can hear construction crews cleaning up the wreckage of the robot attacks of the day before.

"He wants the astronium," Banner insists. The two of you are sitting at a table in his laboratory. The scientist seems tired but excited, eager to solve this mystery. "That much is clear from my talks with him. He kept asking me for the exact amount we had manufactured and the ways in which it is stored. Of course, he told me he wanted it for peaceful industrial development, but now I see that it was all a lie."

"So what does he want the astronium for?" you ask, though you think you already know.

"It's not astronium," Banner explains,

drawing some lines and numbers on a blackboard. "It's the used astronium. After it has neutralized some radioactive material, the astronium itself becomes highly radioactive—and unstable. It would make excellent material for a new kind of atomic weapon."

"Atomic weapons?" you ask. "Is that what this is all about?"

"I think so," Banner replies. "Don't forget that with enough astronium, Doom would have both a weapon and a cure for radiation. He would have a terrible offense and a perfect defense in one package."

"Why can't Doom just make his own?" you ask.

"Because he doesn't have the knowledge," Banner replies as he paces back and forth. "I haven't told anyone the complete process. Also, he doesn't have the materials. You need trace minerals from rare meteorites. No, Doom needs me and he needs the materials we have here to make astronium."

You get up from your seat and stand in Banner's way.

"Look, Doc," you say, "All this has been interesting, and if I ever do a science show on public television, you'll be the first guy I have on as a guest. But we're still not closer to figuring out a way to stop Doom. What do we do? Can we get rid of the stuff? Put it somewhere Doom can't get to it? He had no trouble breaking in here yesterday."

"I have a better idea," Banner says. "I've been working on something—a new process in making astronium. It's a way of stabilizing it so that it cannot be used for weapons. If I can do that, then the astronium we've made will be useless to Doom. And any new astronium will also be useless to him."

"I don't get it," you say, shaking your head. "If you can make astronium harmless, why haven't you done it before now?"

Banner stops and gives you a grave look. "Because it's an experimental process," he says slowly. "Dr. Langkowski said it was too dangerous. He thought it might set off a chain reaction."

"A chain reaction?"

Banner pauses before replying. "An explosion," he says softly. "A big one."

Quickly he sketches some numbers and formulas on the blackboard. He writes so quickly you can scarcely follow, but thanks to your science background, you can pick up the general drift. The process *is* pretty dangerous. It has to be tightly controlled. But Banner seems sure he can make it work.

"I was going to attempt it in a few months," Banner says when he's done. "After we did some more preparation. But now I think I'd better go ahead."

"Wait a minute," you say. "Let's not be hasty. We can try to stop Doom some other way before we . . ."

"No!" Banner interrupts angrily. "This is the

only way to be sure. I will not have an experiment of mine used for evil purposes. I've lived too long with the bad results of another experiment."

His voice trails off but you know what he's talking about. It's the experiment that turned him into the Hulk long ago.

"I'll do anything to keep the astronium from falling into Doom's hands," Banner says quietly. "Just as I would do anything to keep from becoming the Hulk again."

You stare at the scientist with a mixture of pity and awe. He's carrying a heavy load around with him. And you thought *you* had troubles.

Banner seems so sure about this new experiment. But he's been wrong before. What if it goes wrong? Are you ready to take responsibility for a nuclear explosion?

But what if he doesn't go ahead? How are you going to keep Doom away from the astronium? Are you ready to take responibility for letting that madman get his hands on a new weapon? What do you do?

IF YOU TELL BANNER TO PERFORM THE
EXPERIMENT, GO TO CHAPTER 33,
PAGE 8.

IF YOU TELL BANNER NOT TO DO IT,
GO TO CHAPTER 32, PAGE 113.

CHAPTER 43

"Hulk!" you shout, as you swing around, on a web-line, just out of his reach. "That's not Betty!"

"Stupid bug-man!" the Hulk scowls, as he clumsily tries to catch you. "You think that Hulk does not know his friend?"

"If it was Betty," you ask, setting yourself on a collision course with the robot, "could I do this?"

You let go of your web-line and hit the robot with a flying kick right in the head. As you planned, the head snaps off and goes rolling onto the floor. A tangle of wires and electronic parts spills out. Proudly you lift the robot head and show it to the startled Hulk.

"See?" you say, waving it about. "I told you."

You never thought of the Hulk as a sensitive being, but the look of sadness, grief and loss on his face breaks your heart. So does the realization of what he's going to do to you next.

"Arrgh! Bug-man killed Betty!"

In his fury, the Hulk reaches out with both fists and pulls an entire wall of the building out of its foundation. He hurls it at you and reaches for more. Girders and concrete fall around you. The entire place is collapsing around your ears. It's like being in a driving storm, except bricks and steel are falling, instead of rain. You don't see any way to escape. This looks like the end. As the stones keep falling you can only think, "This is what I get for trying to teach an old Hulk new tricks."

THE END

CHAPTER 12

You shoot a web-line to the top of the stage and swing over the robots, flip over and land next to the R.A.D. In a split-second you have the device surrounded in a web-harness. The machine is heavy, but with your spider-strength you can slide it across the floor and out the stage door before the robots have a chance to get any closer.

"Now, if this plan works like I imagined," you think as you move the heavy machine down a hallway, "I'll be able to use the R.A.D. as bait to draw those overgrown wind-up toys away from the crowd to someplace I can deal with them until more help shows up."

"Come on you junk heaps!" you shout over your shoulder. "This is where we separate the men from the machines!"

But to your dismay, when you look back, there are no robots following you. Suddenly you have a very bad feeling that you made the wrong choice. You drop the web-harness and race back to the auditorium. Too late. The robots are gone. You see them flying over the rooftops of the GTC complex. And you can just make out the figure of Bruce Banner being held by one of them.

"They were after *Banner!*" you think, mentally kicking yourself. "They must have knocked him out so he couldn't turn into the Hulk. And I didn't even put a spider-tracer on them!"

You get ready to leap through the blast hole and pursue them, but suddenly there's a figure in your way. It's the security guard. The one who was stunned by the robot. At first you think he wants to thank you, but then you notice he's holding his revolver— and pointing it straight at you!

"D—Don't move, Spider-Man," he stammers.

"But, but they're getting away!" you shout, pointing through the jagged hole at the rapidly disappearing shadows.

"Maybe they are, but you're not," the guard says, a determined look in his eye.

"What are you talking about?" you ask with a sinking feeling.

"We saw you!" he shouts, and several reporters nearby nod in agreement. "We saw you steal the R.A.D. machine. Spider-Man, you're under arrest!"

You start to argue, but you know it's no use. When did anyone ever believe Spider-Man, anyway? And you also know that by the time you straighten the whole mess out and show them where the R.A.D. is, the robots and Banner will be long gone. And it will be too late for you to do anything about it.

THE END

CHAPTER 13

"It's just too chancey," you realize. "With Banner or the Hulk in the mix, anything could happen. I'd better get him and Langkowski out of here first."

Those thoughts race through your mind in the split-second it takes to swoop down on the stage and land next to Banner. You figure it should be easy to grab him, put Langkowski in a web-hammock and get all three of you to safety. You didn't figure on Banner resisting your help.

"Come on, Doc," you say, holding out your hand. He swats it away, angrily.

"Spider-Man!" he shouts, glaring at you. "Are you here to cause trouble, too?"

"Trouble?" you repeat, dumbfounded. "I just want to—"

But you don't get to finish you sentence. Distracted by Banner, you don't pick up on your spider-sense's warning until it's too late. Like a pile driver, the force of the robot's energy beam hits you in the side and drives you thirty feet through the air. You smash into the wall at the back of the stage with a bone-crunching impact.

You must have blacked out because the next thing you know you're awakening at the rear of the stage and the three robots are making their way through the hole in the auditorium wall. The R.A.D. and Langkowski are both where they were moments ago. But an unconscious Bruce Banner is being carried away by the lead robot.

"They must have knocked him out," you realize. "That's why he didn't turn into the Hulk. They were after him all the time."

You struggle to your feet, still pretty woozy. Somehow you manage to make it to the jagged hole before the robots have disappeared. You see now that there are jet thrusters on their legs. One by one they lift off, rising into the air.

"Hey!" you shout, shooting a web-line at the nearest one. "Don't I get a ride, too?"

You snag the robot as it rises above the parking lot and you're lifted off the ground with it. Your mind is still foggy, but your spider-sense gives you just enough warning to swing out of the way of the energy beam as it blasts past you and into the pavement below.

"You missed! No kewpie doll for you!" you say as you web-sling to the next robot. You're trying to reach the one carrying Banner, before it gets any higher. You extend your arm and aim your web-shooter, but before you can complete the swing, you feel the web-line snap.

"They cut it!" you realize as you plummet downward. It's all you can do to twist yourself around and shoot out another line to break your fall. But even as you do, you mange to throw a spider-tracer with the other hand. You watch with grim satisfaction as it catches onto the lead robot.

You land feet first, but just barely. Getting ko'd in the auditorium must have taken more out of you than you thought. All you can do is watch as the three robots jet away, quickly vanishing over the rooftops.

"They have Banner," you say to yourself

as you catch your breath. "And I don't think he's invited to a birthday party."

Still dizzy, you set off painfully to follow them.

GO TO CHAPTER 15, PAGE 121.

CHAPTER 18

What can you do? You can't rescue a guy who doesn't want to be rescued. Can you?

"Did Doom do something to you?" you ask. "Has he blackmailed you?"

"No," Banner replies impatiently. "Nothing like that. Now get out of here before—"

The door to the room flies open and in bursts a heavily-armed Latverian guard.

"Halt!" he commands, waving an automatic rifle at you. He's immediately joined by three other beefy, black-clad goons, each waving his own personal machine gun.

"Who are you guys supposed to be?" you ask, leaping to the ceiling with an easy jump. "Refugees from a bad sci-fi movie?"

The guards take aim at you. But before they

can fire, you've clogged the barrels of their guns with webbing. In another moment you've knocked them down and trussed them up with more webbing. Angrily, you turn to Banner, who hasn't moved at all during the fracas.

"What'd you do, Doc—set off an alarm?" you ask accusingly. "You're working with Doom!"

"No, you don't understand," he says, his face contorted with—what? Fear? Anger? "I didn't . . . I want to . . ."

But you don't get to hear his explanation. Your spider-sense suddenly tingles. Sounds of heavy footsteps outside the door tell you you're about to have company. You leap toward the balcony. But you still can't bring yourself to leave Banner—not yet. There's something very wrong here. You turn in time to see Doom himself stride into the bedroom.

"He's even uglier than his Doombot . . . if that's possible," you think. But for once, you keep your wisecracks to yourself. As for Doom, he's in no mood for kidding around. But then, what else is new?

"I was expecting you, Spider-Man," he says, tilting his steel face mask in your direction.

"You knew I was coming," you snap back, "but did you bake a cake?"

"I do not find your blather amusing," he replies, stiffly. "You are trespassing on Latverian territory and are under arrest."

"Great idea, Doomsy," you say. You point to Banner. "And when you call the police to take me away, don't forget to mention your hostage here."

Doom lifts one of his metal gauntlets as your spider-sense tingles—a sure sign he's about to attack. You dodge sideways as a high-powered energy beam lances out from the palm with the force of a cannon. It pulses past you, blasting the doors, the curtain and part of the balcony out into the night.

"I see you're in the mood for redecorating," you say, as you shoot a web-lasso around Doom's knees. You jerk the web-line hard and Doom stumbles sideways, almost falls. But he's still not down. He raises his other gauntlet.

"Stop!" You realize Banner is screaming. But who is he yelling at? You? Doom? Both of you? You don't have time to worry about it because Doom is firing at you again. You leap easily out of the beam's path and it blows away what's left of the door frame.

"My turn, Doomsy!" you say to the armored villain. "Just keep your eye on the bouncing spider!" You dive to one side, bounce against a wall, leaping up in the air and rebounding off a ceiling fan. Doom is blasting away at you the whole time, but you're moving too fast for him to draw a bead on you. Bouncing against the far wall, you spring onto Doom from behind.

110

Doom is blasting away at you the whole time, but you're moving too fast for him to draw a bead on you.

"Ol' web-head sacks the quarterback at the twenty-yard line and the crowd goes wild!" you crow as you flatten the tin-pot dictator with one punch.

You've got Doom pinned, but not secured. A few web-strands will do it. You're about to finish him off when you spot something out of the corner of your eye. It's Banner. He's reaching for something! What is it? A weapon? Another alarm?

You're confused. You know Banner can act sort of weird sometimes, but he's always been on the right side—at least until now. Still, he said he wasn't a prisoner. Could the whole kidnapping have been a fake? Is this one elaborate trap? Is Bruce Banner really in league with Doc Doom? You only have a split-second to make up your mind.

What do you do?

IF YOU TRY TO STOP BANNER, GO TO CHAPTER 19, PAGE 20.

IF YOU KEEP FIGHTING DOOM, GO TO CHAPTER 20, PAGE 23.

CHAPTER 32

"It's just too risky," you say, trying to sound sure of yourself. "You shouldn't rush into the experiment just because of Doom. For all we know, that's what he has in mind."

Your arguments must make some kind of sense, because Banner reluctantly agrees.

"We just have to make sure that the astronium is someplace where Doom can't get to it," you add. "I don't think General Techtronics is the place."

"I don't know," Banner says with a smile. "I've got it hidden someplace I don't think anyone will ever find it."

"I hope it's not a piggy bank," you reply.

"No, it's a little more hi-tech than that," Banner says. He motions you to follow him. You leave the laboratory and walk down the hall until you're standing in a small kitchenette.

"You hid the astronium in the doughnuts?" you ask, pointing to a box on the counter.

"Even scientists have to eat sometimes," Banner replies.

He walks to the small microwave and begins punching some numbers into the control panel.

"Uh, Bruce," you say, "I know you must be hungry and all, but is this really the time to be making popcorn?"

Banner silences you with a raised hand. It's obvious that the numbers he's entering aren't instructions for defrosting a chicken pot pie. It's some kind of code, or combination or—

With just a whisper of machinery, the entire kitchenette wall lifts off the floor. Behind it is a room-sized vault, with its own fingerprint-controlled security system. You whistle in appreciation.

"Not bad, Doc," you say. "But can it reheat meat loaf?"

"This storage container is undetectable," Banner says proudly. "There is zero radiation leakage. And it doesn't appear on any blueprints or charts of this building. Doom will never find it, unless he tears the place apart brick by brick."

"Which won't be necessary now," says an all-too-familiar voice from behind them. "Thanks to you, Dr. Banner."

It's Doom! Here in General Techtronics. You don't know how he did it, but you don't have time to think about it. You jump straight up, grab hold of the ceiling, flip over and dive straight for him. Funny, he doesn't seem to notice you. Not even when you go right through him!

114

"A hologram?" you say as you roll onto the floor. "But how?"

"No!" Banner cries with anger and disgust. "Doom must have planted something on me when . . ."

"When you were my guest," the hologram finishes the sentence for the surprised scientist.

"And now I've . . ." a shocked Banner begins.

"Shown him where the astronium is," you say.

And he's on his way here right now, you realize, just about the same moment that the roof of the building disappears into thin air.

GO TO CHAPTER 38, PAGE 124.

CHAPTER 37

Reverse? That makes sense. If you want to stop the thing, just make it go in the other direction. You select that option on the computer screen.

A message begins flashing in front of you. REVERSE MECHANISM NOT INSTALLED.

At the same time a large bright red clock appears on the screen.

"Chain reaction has started," says the computer voice. "Time remaining, ten seconds."

Ten seconds! You frantically hit the computer keys, trying to find some other option. But all the computer will do is count off the time remaining. You now have seven seconds until that astronium blows up and takes this whole building with it, including a certain friendly neighborhood Spider-Man!

"Six, five, four . ." the seconds tick off. You hear the mammoth green monster still fighting the robots in the background.

"Hulk smash!" he roars.

At least the Hulk will probably survive, you think as the clock ticks down. For the first and probably the last time in your life you find yourself wishing you were an ugly green monster.

"Three, two, one . . ."

THE END

CHAPTER 45

"That must be the real Doom!" you shout. You point to the figure flying into the sky. You know the General Techtronics complex is surrounded by police and by this time maybe even the army. Doom will want to get back to the safety of the embassy where he can't be questioned or arrested.

"Tin Man can't fly as fast as Hulk can jump!" shouts the mighty green one. He crouches for a moment, then launches himself into the air on muscle power alone.

"I think I'll hitch a ride," you say to yourself. You shoot out a web-line, which catches the Hulk's left heel. You're immediately lifted off the ground. In fact, your weight doesn't even slow the Hulk's rise.

Like a guided missile, the Hulk rises in the air. The figure of Doom grows rapidly as he gets closer and closer. The tall spires of Manhattan spread out below you. About this point you start wondering if you should have trusted the Hulk's judgment. Will he be able to reach Doom? He's good at leaping, but somehow you don't think he ever passed a course in ballistics.

Finally, even the Hulk has to obey gravity. You feel his rise slowing down. Doom is jetting through the air, not even looking back.

"One good thing about Hulk power," you think. "It's silent."

The Hulk is still gaining on the crazed Latverian. Then you see Doom begin to pull away.

"Thanks Hulk," you say. "I'll take it from here."

"Huh?" The Hulk looks puzzled as he begin to drop. He just never did get the hang of Newtonian physics, did he? You know that he won't be hurt by the fall. And now you have some fancy web-slinging to do.

Using your weight to gain some leverage, you swing forward just as the Hulk reaches the peak of his jump. Your swing takes you through the air, almost to Doom. This is the tricky part. You have to let go of your web-line, or be pulled back to earth by the Hulk. At the same time you shoot out another one, which hits Doom square in the back.

He turns, as if this is the first time he knew you were following him.

"You fool!" he shouts. "You'll never stop me!"

You slam into him as he says it. He turns and tries to level his blasters at you, but you've already bound his steel gauntlets and arms in webbing. A few more web-strands and he's securely tied. Doom's jets turn off and the two of you begin to tumble earthward, following the Hulk.

"We'll be killed!" Doom screams. You're dropping like a stone and the streets of Manhattan rush up toward you.

"Hey, it's only a thousand feet or so," you think as you watch the ground come closer. There's no time for a webbing parachute, but you see a likely skyscraper. You shoot out some web-lines, which act like bungee cords. They stretch as they snag the building, slowing your fall. Gripping Doom securely, you fall into an easy web-swinging descent. Finally, you drop almost gently to the pavement with the bound Doctor Doom beside you. Not far away is the crater the Hulk made when he crashed to the ground a few moments earlier.

"Hey, Hulk!" you shout as you see his large green head poke over the edge of the pavement. The Hulk shuffles toward you, brushing pieces of sidewalk out of his hair. A crowd of spectators has gathered, although they're staying a good distance away. In the background you hear police sirens. You can imagine the next morning's headlines.

SPIDER-MAN CAPTURES DOCTOR DOOM, STOPS ATTACK ON GENERAL TECHTRONICS.

"Well, Doom," you gloat to the steel

masked figure on the sidewalk. "Hope you like to have your picture in the paper."

"Yes, you fool," Doom replies. "But the article will read, 'Doctor Doom captures the world's supply of astronium!' "

"Astronium . . ." you repeat dully. You have a sinking feeling in the pit of your stomach. Suddenly it hits you. This isn't the real Doom—it's a Doombot!

"Yes, you fool!" the Doombot says. "While you were chasing this robot, I was stealing the astronium from General Techtronics! Now all the astronium in the world is mine. When I have created my astronium bomb, the world will be at my feet! You and all the other pitiful creatures who have opposed me will bow down before my power!"

You sit on the pavement, exhausted. After all this, you let Doom get away with the astronium! By now, he's probably on his way to Latveria with it. The world is in big trouble and all because you made the wrong choice.

There's a dull crackle and then a small pop. The Doombot's face mask falls away to reveal the robot's electronic circuits.

The Hulk has come up beside you. He stares down at the lifeless robot.

"Not real Tin Man?" he asks.

"No, Hulk," you say slowly. "Not real Tin Man."

"Bug-man follow wrong Tin Man," the Hulk grunts. "Stupid bug-man!"

"Yes, Hulk," you agree. "Stupid bug-man."

THE END

CHAPTER 15

The buzzing of your spider-sense is constant as you web-sling high over the city rooftops, following the signal of your spider-tracer. Pretty soon you should have the strange robots and their victim in sight.

As usual, the rhythm of swinging into action from one web-line to another, over and again, has calmed you down. The sun is setting and a blanket of darkness has fallen over the big city, making everything seem peaceful. Web-slinging is so much like flying that you can't help enjoying yourself. In fact, for a moment you almost forget what has brought you out on this beautiful evening.

Your spider-sense's tingling increases as you travel northward on Fifth Avenue. You continue on until you reach a block of buildings across the street from Central Park. Then you see it. It must have been in the back of your mind all along, because somehow you're just not that surprised. Of course. Who else would be able to build such high-tech robots and then use them for a nasty deed like kidnapping a famous scientist? It had to be him, and now you're sure of it. Because there, right in your path, is the Latverian Embassy—home to that brilliant madman, Doctor Doom.

You swing easily into some treetops not far from the embassy compound. You pause just to make sure that you're on the right track, but there's really no doubt in your mind. The tracer signals are coming from inside the mansion. Doctor Doom has kidnapped Bruce Banner.

Why? With a madman like Doom, it's impossible to tell. But it makes sense in a twisted way. Doom is a brilliant scientist himself. More likely than not, he plans to force Banner to work on some new weapon or device. Doom is always working on some new gizmo he hopes will bring him what he craves most—enough power to rule the world.

"Doom is the kind of guy who definitely needs to get a life," you think as you slip out of the tree and swing toward the embassy fence. You've tangled with Doom many times before and it's never been much fun. Of all the super-villains you've come up against, he's certainly the cleverest . . . and the most dangerous.

But this time, you think, you have a real advantage. There's no way Doom could have planned on Spider-Man being at General

Techtronics when he sent his robots to snatch Banner. With any luck, you should be able to take him by surprise.

Now the shadows help you blend in as you land, cat-like, in a tree just above the embassy wall. You've had enough encounters with Doom to know to look for some pretty sophisticated sensors around the embassy.

And there they are. Tiny strobing lights along the wall show you where the heat-detecting infra-red "eyes" are hidden. Springing from the tree, you evade the "eyes" by jumping above their sensor range. A moment later and you're on the other side of the wall, your feet pressed firmly against the side.

And there you stop, thunderstruck, staring at the courtyard below. You can't believe your eyes. There he is—Doctor Doom himself in his green cloak and steely gray mask. He's pacing up and down, almost as if he's waiting for someone. But there isn't anyone else around.

This is your chance to take him out, you realize. But maybe you should rescue Banner first.

What do you do?

IF YOU ATTACK DOOM, GO TO
CHAPTER 16, PAGE 57.

IF YOU LOOK FOR BANNER, GO TO
CHAPTER 17, PAGE 131.

CHAPTER 38

The hall is flooded with bright sunlight. In the sky above you is a fleet of flying vehicles, each one carrying a different robot. There must be a dozen of them. And in the center of them all is Doctor Doom. He's wearing some kind of jet pack and he floats just above you, taunting you and Banner both.

"Fools!" he cries. "You have done exactly as I planned. You have led me right to the astronium!"

"It's no good to you without my help!" Banner shouts. The explosion and the sight of Doom have gotten him frightened and angry. He's already dangerously close to his breaking point. A little more and he'll transform into the Hulk!

"You can't use the astronium without me!" the scientist repeats. "Only I know how to control it!"

"You over-estimate your value," Doom responds. His steel mask shines in the sunlight. "I don't need you. I never needed you. All I need is the astronium and—the Hulk!"

"The Hulk!" Banner is shocked into silence. You figure this would be a good time to put in your two cents.

"Hey Doom," you shout. "You must have a few screws loose in that tin can you call a head. The Hulk will dump you in the nearest recycling bin!"

"As usual, arachnid, you show your pitiful lack of brain power," Doom replies. "I have a plan for the Hulk. And now that I have learned where the astronium is, it is time for my plan to begin!"

He levels a steel gauntlet directly at Banner.

"Watch it!" you shout. You leap at the startled scientist and get both of you clear just in time. A blast of raw energy hits the floor where Banner had been standing.

"He doesn't want to hurt him," you realize, "just cause enough pain to turn him into the Hulk. That's why he hasn't set his robots loose. But why does he want the Hulk? How can he control him?"

You don't have time to think it over.

"Get out of here," you tell Banner. "I'll cover you!"

"No!" Banner insists. "I can't let Doom get to the astronium!"

Why doesn't anyone ever listen to you? You look up and Doom and his robots have flown lower. You have one chance, maybe. Doom is aiming his gauntlet at you and Banner for another shot. You shoot a web-line for the robot nearest Doom. With a running leap, you launch yourself forward, putting all your weight into the swing. It works! You've jerked the robot off-balance and it's headed right for Doom!

But not in time. Doom manages to get off another blast just as he gets run down by his own robot. The beam goes wild, striking Banner in his side and shoulder.

"YEOW!" he screams in pain. Too late, you swing back to his side. You're only in time to watch as his skin and body begin to shift and change. In a matter of seconds he has transformed from a human of average height and build to a mammoth, seven-foot tall, rampaging green Goliath with muscles like tree trunks.

"Who hurt Hulk?!"

You step back. Too late. The giant green brute stares at you. He seems to be searching his memory, puzzling out what has happened to him.

"Bug-man!" he shouts, waving a fist that seems to be the size of a washing machine. "Did Bug-man hurt Hulk?"

"No, Hulk," you say soothingly tired of being called "bug-man." "It wasn't me. It was Doom."

"Doom?" The Hulk looks even more confused, if that's possible.

"Look, Hulk," you say, pointing up. "Look up in the sky."

The Hulk looks up and you follow his gaze. Maybe this will work, you think. Maybe the Hulk will attack Doom. But where is Doom? And all those robots? Somehow they've all disappeared. But they can't have flown away so quickly. It's some kind of trick, an optical illusion that Doom has produced. Doom and his robots must still be there, only you just can't see them. What's even worse is the Hulk can't see them, either.

"No Doom!" the Hulk says, taking a threatening step forward. "Bug-man try to trick Hulk! It was bug-man that shot Hulk!

"No, Hulk, it wasn't me," you say, backing up even more. But it does no good. The Hulk lowers his massive head and charges you like some mutant green bull. What are you going to do now? Fighting the Hulk is not much of an option. But neither is trying to explain what happened. You can try to lure the Hulk away and see if you can lose him. But what about Doom? He's still here, somewhere. While you're playing tag with the Hulk, the crazed dictator will be free to put his plans into action. Maybe you can somehow get the Hulk to see Doom. But how can you do that?

IF YOU TRY TO GET AWAY FROM THE HULK, GO TO CHAPTER 39, PAGE 145.

IF YOU TRY TO EXPLAIN THINGS TO THE HULK, GO TO CHAPTER 38A, PAGE 134.

CHAPTER 27

"*A*rrgh!*"

With an ear-splitting growl, the Hulk sweeps the room with his fist, shattering equipment, turning over tables and incidentally knocking over the chair you which holds you fast. The electronic shackles spring open and you roll free, making sure you're out of the Hulk's range. But he hasn't noticed you yet.

"Where is Hulk?" the green behemoth is screaming. "Who put Hulk in stupid chair? Hulk will smash!"

You don't see Doom anywhere. The evil genius must have fled. He claimed to have some way of controlling the Hulk, but obviously it isn't working. Now it's up to you to—to do what, you wonder?

The Hulk turns furiously, striking out again in a blind rage. He hurls a wall of cabinets in your direction. You leap for the ceiling and hang there.

"Bug-man!" the Hulk shouts when he sees you. "Did bug-man bring Hulk here?"

"Yes, it was me!"

For a second, you think you're hearing things. Was that *you* who just answered the Hulk?

"It was me, Spider-Man!" you hear yourself saying. You twist around looking for the source of the voice. Then you see it—another you—standing in the doorway. Things keep getting weirder and weirder.

"*Two* bug-men?" says the Hulk. He scratches his head in confusion.

"I've brought you here to destroy you, Hulk!" says the other Spider-Man.

He steps into the room. As he does, you see the cloaked figure of Doctor Doom just outside. Of course! It's another of Doom's robots!

"Great," you think. "Now that *I've* got it figured out, how do I explain it to pea brain?"

"Don't listen to him, Hulk!" you shout. But then you don't have the faintest idea of what else to add. You can only watch as the Hulk becomes more confused.

"Why does bug-man want to destroy Hulk?" asks the jade giant.

"Because you're a monster, Hulk—a freak!" the robot Spider-Man says. "You don't deserve to live!"

"Don't listen to him, Hulk!" you plead. "*I'm* the real Spider-Man. I mean, the real bug-man! I'm your friend! That's just a robot! It's being controlled by Doctor Doom!"

Hulk peers at you intently, then looks around the room.

"Hulk doesn't see any Doctor Doom!" he says, puzzled.

It's true—Doctor Doom has moved out of sight. He must be controlling the robot from some other place in the dungeon.

"Bug-man tries to trick Hulk!" the Hulk shouts, losing his very short patience.

"Yes, Hulk, I tricked you!" the robot echoes with a taunting laugh. "Because you're an idiot!"

"No!" you plead. "Don't listen to that thing!"

For the moment the green brute stands between you and the robot, clearly trying to make up his mind as to which one to smash first. But you know it won't take long for him to make up his mind, mainly because he doesn't have much mind to make up.

What are you going to do? How can you convince him you're the real bug-man? You can't even convince him that you're not a real bug! But there has to be some way to get through to him. The only other option is to try to escape. But you're still in Doom's dungeon, so that doesn't seem like much of an option, either.

Either way, you have about half a millisecond to decide.

IF YOU TRY TO ESCAPE, GO TO CHAPTER 29, PAGE 21.

IF YOU TRY TO TALK THE HULK OUT OF ATTACKING YOU, GO TO CHAPTER 28, PAGE 149.

CHAPTER 17

"**Y**eehaa!" you gloat. "Doom's a sitting duck and I'm going to knock him down and win a kewpie doll."

You're just about to launch yourself into space and drop down on the unsuspecting tyrant when something stops you.

It's just too easy, isn't it? You show up here, and the very first thing you see is Doom, just waiting in the courtyard for you to sucker-punch him.

"There's something wrong with this picture," you think, hugging the wall even closer. "But what is it?" A few seconds later, you get your answer. A trio of soldiers, dressed in the midnight black of Doom's Latverian Guard marches across the courtyard, their boots echoing off the flagstones. But none of them salutes, or so much as looks at the form of the fearsome dictator. They walk by it and disappear through a door on the far side.

"If that was the real Doom," you realize, "those lackeys would be dead right about now. No one, and I mean *no one* ignores Doctor Doom and lives to tell about it. That must be one of Doom's robots—his Doombots."

That was a close call and it's left you a little shook up. But you still have a scientist to rescue, so you set about finding him. Hugging the shadows you make your way along the wall and over to the mansion itself. You know that in his own twisted way, Doom likes to pride himself on his "hospitality." There's a good chance that Banner isn't being held in a prison cell but in one of the fancy rooms inside.

And it doesn't take you long to find which one. You step noiselessly onto a broad balcony and peer through the wide French doors. There is Bruce Banner, sitting calmly at an ornately carved desk. He doesn't act like a guy who's just been kidnapped by killer robots. Maybe he's a robot himself. Another trap, like the Doombot? You sneak up to get a closer look.

No, it's Banner all right. Your spider-sense would have warned you if it wasn't the real scientist. You check the doors for any alarms and to your surprise you find none. So you just push them open and walk in.

"Doc," you whisper. "Come on."

Banner turns immediately and stares at you in shock.

"Spider-Man!" he says, sounding annoyed. "What are you doing here?"

"Looks like a rescue attempt to me, Doc,"

you reply. You wish he would keep his voice lower. "By the way, this is where you're supposed to thank me."

"Thank you?" Banner looks at you like you've lost your marbles. "But I don't want to be rescued. Get out of here, before you start trouble."

Every now and then, even a genuine card-carrying super hero is speechless, and this is one of those times. Banner doesn't want to be rescued? What's going on here? Has he been brainwashed? There hasn't been enough time for that. And what are you supposed to do now? Just turn around and leave? Or do you rescue him in spite of himself?

What do you do?

IF YOU LEAVE, GO TO CHAPTER 18, PAGE 108.

IF YOU TRY TO RESCUE BANNER, GO TO CHAPTER 21, PAGE 148.

CHAPTER 38A

The Hulk charges and you crawl up the wall behind you. The green goliath strikes the wall head-on, driving his skull through the concrete until he's buried up to his neck. You use the opportunity to drop down onto his wide green shoulders. It's a dangerous move, but you want to make sure the Hulk goes where you want him to.

Even though the sky above the wrecked building *looks* empty, you know it can't be. Doom and his robots have got to be there. It's just an optical illusion that makes them invisible. You're not sure how the twisted genius is doing it, but you think you know a way to get around the trick.

"Look, Hulk," you say, as you balance on his shoulders. "No use pounding your head against the wall. I'm not the bad guy here. It's Doom!"

He pulls his head out of the wall and shakes the dust and bricks out of his hair. You leap to the safety of a diferent corner.

"No Doom here!" the Hulk insists. "Bug-man try to trick Hulk. Hulk not stupid. Stupid bug-man is stupid!"

"Stupid bug-man may be stupid," you agree. "But he's Hulk's friend. You want to see Doom, then come on!"

"Nothing there!" the Hulk shouts and he charges you again.

You shoot a web-line to the highest point still standing in the roofless building. Leaping into space you hurl yourself to the furthest limits of your swing and then let go, flying upward like a stone out of a slingshot.

"Bug-man can't get away from Hulk!" you hear him shout.

The Hulk braces his legs against the floor and jumps straight up. It's a very small jump by Hulk standards—only forty feet in the air. But it's enough to get him to where he can almost reach out and grab you. *And* where he can see Doctor Doom and his fleet of robots hovering in the air all around. Just as you suspected, Doom's disappearing act only worked from below. Once you and the Hulk were up on his level, you could see him plain as day.

"Tin Man!" the Hulk shouts, forgetting all about you. "Bug-man told the truth!"

In an amazing act of agility, the Hulk manages to twist himself in mid-air and lunge for Doom. But gravity pulls the both of you back to earth before he can do any damage. You break your fall with a few well-placed web-lines. The Hulk breaks his fall by, well, *breaking* things.

135

Now you can see the Doom army quite clearly and so can the Hulk. The giant green creature is pulling himself out of the wreckage of the laboratory. He's about to leap up again. You're feeling pretty good about things.

"Let Doom handle the Hulk *now*," you think.

Doom descends to the ground. Somehow he doesn't seem worried at all.

GO TO CHAPTER 40, PAGE 40.

CHAPTER 34

Who knows what a raging Hulk will do in a scene like this? Your mind is filled with pictures of astronium scattered to the winds by a rampaging green brute. If you can just get Banner out of here, you might be able to get back in time to stop the experiment and stop Doom's robots. It's your only chance.

The robots have moved apart, trying to get you in a cross fire. In the split-second before they fire, you grab Banner and swing up on a web-line. In a flash, you're over the robots and out of the lab, carrying the wounded scientist in your arms like a child. He's still in pain and furious, but the worst has passed—he's not turning into the Hulk.

Less than a minute later you have Banner outside on a grassy hill by the parking lot. From the sounds coming from inside, you can tell that the police have arrived to fight with the robots. Maybe there's time to get back and stop them. Then you hear the alarm—high-pitched, insistent, one you haven't heard before.

"What's that?" you ask Banner. You're afraid to hear the answer.

"It's the experiment!" he says with a look of terror on his face. "A chain reaction!"

Immediately people come streaming out of the buildings all around you. They run in all directions, trying to get away. You jump to your feet. Maybe there's still time, maybe you can shut it down before it blows!

"No!" Banner shouts, grabbing your arm before you can dash back inside. "There are only seconds left! You'll be vaporized!"

"But I—" you start to say.

Suddenly the world becomes very, very bright as if someone was shining a powerful searchlight right into your pupils. You're blinded for just a second. The pain is intense, but brief. It's followed immediately by a roar like a waterfall. Except this waterfall is going up. Blinking away the glare, you see an entire

137

building rise into the air and scatter into pieces. The ground shakes and heaves. You throw yourself down as the blast of the shock wave washes over you.

Later, you manage to sort it all out. Miraculously, no one was killed in the explosion. Somehow everyone got out in time. Except for the robots, which you figure are now up in the great junkyard in the sky. But the astronium is gone, blown into microscopic bits and throw into the atmosphere. That means that everyone in New York has had a chance to breathe some of the stuff. Bruce Banner thinks that the amount was too small to cause harm to people, but no one knows for sure. The papers have been running the story for a week now.

SPIDER-MAN WRECKS EXPERIMENT
ENVIRONMENTAL DISASTER FEARED
Even Banner blames you.

"You should have left me there," he accuses you. "I could have shut it down in time."

There's no use telling him he was about to become the Hulk. There's no use explaining about the robots. After all he's only saying things that you've thought yourself. Somehow, once again, things have gone wrong and Spider-Man is to blame. It's just not fair. You're going to have to live with this for a very long time.

THE END

CHAPTER 25

Banner has too much of a hair trigger temper. You know from past experience that it doesn't take much to set off a transformation into the Hulk. You raise both hands, palms forward, and back up.

"Okay, Doc," you say softly. "I'm going. I don't want to force you to do anything. I just thought you were kidnapped. In trouble. I wanted to help."

Banner's face relaxes. He slumps back in the chair.

"That's okay," he says. "For a while there, I thought I was kidnapped, myself."

You don't want to get him angry again, but you can't help yourself. "You mean, you're staying here of your own free will?"

"Doom says I'm free to go. He says those robots were malfunctioning. They were supposed to just invite me here for a meeting."

"Some invitation," you reply. "Hasn't he ever heard of E-mail?"

Banner shoots you a look of annoyance. "He showed me their programming. It *was* a malfunction!"

"Okay, I believe you," you say, even

though you don't. "But, if you don't mind my asking, and I'm not trying to judge you, so please don't take this the wrong way, but why do you want to stay here with a creep like Doom?"

Banner frowns, but he doesn't react angrily. In fact, it seems like he's trying to figure out the answer even as he tells it to you.

"He says he wants me to help develop commercial uses for astronium," he says, haltingly.

"Is that a fact?" you say, not believing it for a second.

"Yes." Banner nods wearily. "It could open up a whole new area of technology. And Doom is in a unique position to do that."

"He's also in a unique position to use it to take over the world," you counter.

"Not if I'm watching him," Banner replies. "I can be a watchdog, an observer to make sure that Latverian use of astronium is only for peaceful purposes. And Doom promises that a percentage of all his profits will go toward raising the standard of living of his people. Those are the terms of our deal. This could be their chance for a better life."

"But what makes you think a liar like Doom will keep his word?" you protest.

"Because he stands to make millions, maybe billions," Banner replies. "He can afford to give some of that to his people to keep things running smoothly and to keep me working for him."

"And that's it?" you ask. "You're doing it to help the Latverians?"

"No," Banner says slowly. "I admit I have a selfish reason, also." He pauses to take a breath. "Doom says he knows a way to use astronium to keep me from becoming the Hulk . . . ever again."

"Look, Doc," you say urgently, "I know you're a good guy. I can see why you'd want to go along with all this. But you can't trust Doom—believe me. I've faced the guy umpteen times, and he's a psycho."

"I don't know," Banner puts his head in his hands. He seems overcome by weariness. "To tell you the truth, I just don't know. At first, it seemed like a good idea. But now I'm having second thoughts. This has all happened so fast. I need to rest, think it over."

"But not here," you say. "Let me get you out of here. I'll take you back to General Techtronics or anyplace you name. If you change your mind in the morning and decide you want to go through with it, you can always come back." You hope however, that Banner won't.

"No." Banner shakes his head. "If Doom is up to something, and he probably is, I don't want him to know how suspicious I am. Maybe I should stay here. I can be on my guard, try to find out what he's really up to."

"Bad idea," you say. "You could disappear and never be seen again."

"I'm tougher than that," Banner says, with a grim smile. "After all, I live with the Hulk. If Doom is planning to use astronium for some evil scheme, then I *have* to stay and find out what it is."

Banner is a brilliant, resourceful man. And he's right—it would be good to know what Doom was up to *before* he springs his next plot. But can Banner really stand up to a maniac like Doctor Doom? You're not sure.

Do you agree with Banner's plan?

IF YOU AGREE TO LEAVE BANNER THERE, GO TO CHAPTER 26, PAGE 48.

IF YOU DON'T AGREE, GO TO CHAPTER 30, PAGE 144.

CHAPTER 24

It's no good. The Hulk is already warming up to smash the place and the Latverian guards are ready to fire. There's no way you can deal with them both. Even a happy-go-lucky super hero like yourself has to know when it's time to beat a hasty retreat.

You dive for the balcony railing even as you hear the click of the bolts on the guards' rifles.

"Hasta la vista, Greenie!" you shout as you launch yourself into space.

"Hasta?" the Hulk shouts dumbly. "Why does bug-man try to annoy Hulk with stupid words?"

Rat-tat-tat!

The sound of rifle fire is mixed with the thunderous noise of the Hulk tearing apart the mansion wall as he turns his attention to his attackers. You leave it all behind you as you web-sling over the embassy wall and into the safety of the night.

"Let them deal with each other," you say with grim satisfaction. "I still have to figure out what Banner was doing there. Guess I should start by checking out General Techtronics."

You swing through the late night stillness of the city, intent upon your new destination.

GO TO CHAPTER 41, PAGE 77.

CHAPTER 30

"**D**oc," you say, "it's too dangerous. You're a smart guy. A brilliant guy. But you have to be brilliant and twisted and sick to figure out a psycho like Doom. He's got something up his sleeve, believe me."

Banner looks at you and for the first time, he seems completely calm.

"You're right," he says. "I guess it was just wishful thinking. Doom seemed like he really meant what he was saying."

"Hey, it could happen to anyone," you joke. "Come on, let's get out of here."

Banner stands up and you quickly spin a harness out of webbing for him. It's a little awkward with him strapped to your back, but nothing your spider-strength can't handle. Soon the two of you are web-slinging out of the embassy compound.

"It all seems a little too easy," you think as you carry Banner back toward General Techtronics. "Doom isn't usually this careless. But who knows? After all, everyone has an off day, even psycho dictators."

You try to shrug it off as you swing over

the rooftops. But something tells you you haven't finished with Doom—not by a long shot.

GO TO CHAPTER 31, PAGE 98.

CHAPTER 39

You've tried reasoning with the Hulk before. It does as much good as reasoning with a volcano or an earthquake. And you can't have him loose where he might spread the astronium all over Manhattan. Your only chance is to get him away from there, and then to get back as quickly as you can.

"Hey, Hulk!" you shout. You launch yourself with a web-line and swing around the lumbering brute. As you fly past him, you slap his broad green shoulder with the flat of your hand. Of course, the Hulk barely feels it, but even through your glove, your palm stings from hitting his rough, rock-hard skin.

"Tag! You're it!" you cry. You swing away, flipping over the ruined wall. A quick backward glance confirms that the Hulk is bounding after you.

"Puny bug-man!" the green gargantuan comments in his own perceptive way. "Why do you bother Hulk?"

The Hulk reaches out to grab you, but you manage to avoid his tremendous hands. Even though he could easily out-jump you, you're just a little too fast for him to get his fingers around. You lead him over to the General Techtronic buildings and around the vast parking lots, until you reach the edge of a large park.

The Hulk never gets tired, but he does get bored. He stops and angrily kicks a 100-foot oak tree growing at the edge of the complex. The massive tree topples with a thundering crash.

"Stupid bug-man!" the slow-witted creature yells at you. "Hulk does not want to play games! Hulk just wants to be left alone!"

He crouches on his mammoth legs and launches himself into space, like a squat green missile. His leap carries him a half-mile from you. Jumping again and again, the Hulk soon disappears over the horizon.

Without a backward glance you take off toward the wrecked lab, now far on the other side of the General Techtronics complex. The silence hanging over the place doesn't give you much peace. As you land softly inside what remains of the lab, you see that what you feared has happened. Dr. Langkowski, several security guards and two New York City policemen are standing there, surveying the wreckage. The entire vault containing the astronium is gone. Doctor Doom has gotten away with it.

You had known this might happen. But at least you stopped the Hulk from breaking open the vault and starting an environmental disaster. And now you can concentrate on catching Doom. You're about to leap away to pick up his trail, when Dr. Langkowski steps forward. He's probably going to thank you.

"That's okay," you say, waving him off. "I was just—"

You were about to say lucky. But then, maybe you're *not* so lucky. Langkowski points an accusing finger at you.

"Officers!" he demands. "Arrest Spider-Man. He stole the astronium. And he caused the Hulk to wreck our facility!"

You're so stunned that you give the police time to move in and grab you. Of course, you could get free, but how would it look if Spider-Man roughed up some of New York City's finest? You realize that by the time you clear all this up, Doom will be far away. You've failed. You let Doctor Doom get his hands on a terrible weapon.

As they put you in the police car for the ride downtown, all you can think is, "I shoulda gone swimming."

THE END

CHAPTER 21

Something has to be wrong. Banner would never work with Doom of his own free will. Plus you *saw* the guy being kidnapped. The scientist must be brainwashed or drugged, or both.

You walk across the room, trying not to come on too strong. After all, you know what happens when Banner gets too excited.

"Come on," you say. "You're not feeling well. Let me get you out of here."

You place your hand on his arm. He jerks it away, angrily.

"Leave me alone!" he demands.

This is a real problem. Of course, you could force Banner to go with you. As long as he stays as Banner. But can you get him out of there without getting him so angry he turns into the Hulk? Banner has been able to keep himself under control through all of this. He ought to be able to listen to reason. Then again, you can never predict what will happen with him. You hesitate, unsure of your next move.

> IF YOU LEAVE BANNER ALONE, GO TO
> CHAPTER 25, PAGE 139.
>
> IF YOU TRY TO GET HIM TO LEAVE
> WITH YOU, GO TO CHAPTER 22,
> PAGE 43.

CHAPTER 28

You can't prove you're the real Spidey, but at least you can get the Hulk to see there's something fishy going on. Hulk may be dumb, you think, but he's not that dumb. If he sees *two* Spider-Men, side-by-side, maybe he'll get the idea that something's wrong. Then there's a chance he won't listen to that robot.

"Hulk!" you shout, as you swing around on a web-line, just out of his reach. "How can there be two bug-men?"

You land near the robot, staying on guard from attack.

"Hulk does not know." The Hulk stares at

you dumbly. Then he looks at the robot Spider-Man. He seems genuinely puzzled. For a moment you think maybe something has seeped through that thick skull of his. The Hulk opens his mouth.

"Bug-man tries to confuse Hulk!" he roars in frustration. "Wants to destroy Hulk! But Hulk will destroy bug-man first!"

In his fury, the Hulk jumps up with both fists raised and pulls the stone ceiling of the dungeon down on the both of you. Boulders and stones fall around you. The entire place is collapsing around your ears. You don't see any way to escape. This looks like the end. As the stones keep falling you can only think, "I guess he really *is* that dumb."

THE END

You are Peter Parker, the amazing Spider-Man. The Sinister Six attack, led by your archenemy, Dr. Octopus. You must face and defeat The Chameleon, the Hobgoblin, Mysterio, the Shocker and the Vulture. Then you must overcome Doc Ock himself — the one man who knows there's a connection between Peter Parker and Spider-Man! And now *you* could win this fully animated, three-dimensional, action packed interactive adventure just by entering the Sweepstakes for a Spider-Man® CD-ROM.

CLIMB HIGHER THAN EVER BEFORE. ENTER TO WIN A SPIDER-MAN® CD-ROM!

AN ARCHWAY PAPERBACK

500 Grand Prizes:

Spider-Man®: The Sinister Six™: an interactive CD-ROM game based on the Marvel Comics® super-hero.

Name _____

Birthdate _____

Address _____

City_____ State ____ Zip _____

Phone _____

ARCHWAY PAPERBACKS SPIDER-MAN® SWEEPSTAKES
Official Rules:

1. No Purchase Necessary. Enter by submitting the completed Official Entry Form or by sending on a 3" x 5" card on which you have written your name, address, and a daytime telephone number to the Spider-Man Sweepstakes, 1230 Sixth Ave., 13th floor, New York, NY 10020. Entries must be received by 12/31/97. Not responsible for postage due, lost, late, illegible, stolen, incomplete, mutilated or misdirected mail. Enter as often as you wish, but one entry per envelope. 500 winners will be selected at random from all eligible entries received in a drawing to be held on or about 12/31/97.

2. Prizes: 500 Spider-Man: The Sinister Six CD-ROMs (approximate retail value: $39.95 each).

3. The sweepstakes is open to legal residents of the U.S. and Canada (except Quebec). Prizes will be awarded to a winner's parent or legal guardian if winner is under 18. Void in Puerto Rico and wherever prohibited by law. Employees, their immediate family members and others living in their household of Simon & Schuster, Inc., Viacom International, Inc., Byron Preiss Multimedia Company, Inc., and Marvel Entertainment Group, Inc. and their respective suppliers, affiliates, divisions, and agencies are not eligible. Prizes are not transferable and may not be substituted except by sponsor for reason of unavailability in which case a prize of equal or greater value will be awarded. One prize per household. The odds of winning a prize depend upon the number of eligible entries received. All prizes will be awarded.

4. If a winner is a Canadian resident, then he/she must correctly answer a time-limited, skill-based question administered by mail.

5. By participating, entrants agree to these rules and decisions of the judges which are final in all respects. Each winner may be required to execute and return an affidavit of eligibility and publicity/liability release within 15 days of notification attempt or an alternative winner may be selected.

6. Simon & Schuster, Inc., Viacom International, Inc., Byron Preiss Multimedia Company, Inc., and Marvel Entertainment Group, Inc. shall have no liability for any injury, loss, or damage of any kind, including without limitation, property damage, personal injury and/or death, arising out of any participation in this sweepstakes or acceptance or use of the prize.

7. All expenses on the receipt and use of the prize, and all federal, state and local taxes are the responsibility of the winners. Winners will be notified by mail. By accepting a prize, winners grant Archway Paperbacks the right to use their names, likenesses, and entries for any advertising, promotion and publicity purposes without further compensation or permission, except where prohibited by law. For a list of prize winners (available after 12/31/97) send a stamped, self-addressed envelope by 1/31/98, to Prize Winners, Archway Paperbacks/Spider-Man Sweepstakes, 13th Floor, 1230 Avenue of the Americas, NY, NY 10020.

Spider-Man® is a trademark and copyright of Marvel Characters, Inc.